Hope for a Better World

Growing Up Quaker in the Midwest

James Walton Blackburn PhD

ISBN 978-1-64299-791-0 (paperback)
ISBN 978-1-64299-792-7 (digital)

Christian Faith Publishing, Inc.
832 Park Avenue
Meadville, PA 16335
www.christianfaithpublishing.com

Printed in the United States of America

I WAS MAD, MAD, mad! And suddenly, *crunch!* I had smashed my fist into my mirror. "Oh my gosh!" But Mother never said a word to me. *Ever.*

Why was a little Quaker boy of eight so upset? It was 1943. Our neighbor, Larry, had tossed a toy tommy gun into our yard. I grabbed it with glee and turned a little crank: "Tat, tat, tat, tat, tat, tat, tat!" What power I felt as I mowed down enemy soldiers.

Then: "Walton!" Mother called me and sent me up to my room.

Mother and Daddy were Wilburite Quakers. I had often heard them talk about the War. War is wrong! Quakers take seriously the commandments "Love your enemies" and "Thou shalt not kill."

This Book

THIS BOOK TELLS THE story of how I grew up in a Wilburite Quaker family in Ohio and attended Scattergood Friends School in Iowa. Here I give an overview of Quakers who originated as the Religious Society of Friends in seventeenth-century England. This is about Wilburite "Friends," who are much different from most Quakers. Their practices are close to early English Friends. I share how the Blackburn Family lived out Quaker beliefs. I tell about Scattergood Friends School in Iowa. I present my personal faith.

An inspiration for this book is *A Quaker Book of Wisdom – Life Lessons in Simplicity, Service, and Common Sense* by Robert Lawrence Smith. He states, "It is my ever-growing conviction that the compassionate Quaker message badly needs to be heard in today's complex, materialistic, often unjust, and discriminatory society. Every day brings new public debate over issues Quakers have always addressed: war and peace, social justice, education, health care, poverty, business ethics, public service, the use of world resources" (Smith 1998, xii–xiii).

Section 1

The Quakers

THE QUAKERS, OR THE Religious Society of Friends, originated in England in the seventeenth century. Two characteristics of Quakers are their stand against war, as taught by Jesus in the New Testament, and their belief in "that of God in every person." They believe each human being has personal access to God through the Inner Light, which "enlightens every person."

The early Quakers had an apostolic fervor that "God was pushing them out to be bearers of a new and mighty word of Life which was to remake the world, a campaign of spiritual conquest" (Jones 2004, xiii). William Penn, founder of Pennsylvania, said Quakerism was "primitive Christianity revived."

They felt their message would change the world just as the message of the Apostles changed the world. "They lived under the sense of 'end time,' as did the early New Testament Christians, which accounted for their sense of urgency about their mission" (Cooper 2000, 168).

Snapshot

In A *Quaker Book of Wisdom*, Robert Lawrence Smith, former headmaster of Sidwell Friends School, gives an amusing snapshot of Quakers.

> Quakerism is the only faith that is most commonly explained in a cascade of negatives. Quakerism has no theology, no body of religious dogma, no sacred books, no written creed. Traditional Quaker worship does not involve a minister, priest or other religious leader. There is no liturgy. There are no crucifixes or other religious images in Quaker Meetinghouses or homes. (Smith 1998, 18)

In a world of chaos and international conflict, the Quakers have a faith that offers great hope to a torn and troubled world. They believe that each person has access to God through the Inner Light, which "enlightens every person in the world." They look to John 1:9, "He was the true light that enlightens everyone coming into the world." (The Holy Bible, New Revised Standard Version 1989).

Quakers take seriously the admonition of Jesus to "love your enemies" and His statement "Blessed are the peacemakers." They feel that the way of the cross of Jesus is entirely inconsistent with war or preparation for war.

Broader Picture

Whalen presents a broader picture. A personal commitment to God and humanity distinguishes Quakers.

> The Quaker worships God by serving Him and through society. Although decidedly mystical, Quakerism does not understand a purely interior religion. It believes that the Christian faith must express itself in action and service. The Quaker tries to seek direct divine illumination by jettisoning all the Christian sacraments, rituals, hymns, formal prayers, and priesthood. The Quaker tries to live by the Inner Light. The Inner Light is not conscience but it is that which enlightens conscience. Quaker theologians

usually describe the Inner Light as 'that of God in each man.' People discern the Inner Light when they silently and patiently wait for God to speak to them. Such direct illumination is far superior to the written revelation of the Bible or Tradition of the church, in the Quaker view. (Whalen 1991, 6)

George Fox and the Quaker Movement

The Religions Society of Friends, or Quakers, originated in the seventeenth century in the midst of the English Civil War when there was great religious, economic and political turmoil. (Cooper 2000, 2)

The Quakers in Iowa, who founded Scattergood Friends School, were Wilburites. They still maintain the silent meditation of the traditional Quaker Meeting for Worship in which everyone waits for an inspirational message from God, or the Holy Spirit. This style was practiced in the Quaker Colony of Pennsylvania founded by William Penn.

George Fox (1624–1691) is often described as the founder of the Friends (Whalen 1991, 6).

Although some suggest that Fox's personality defined the Quaker movement, Barbour states that many early Friends went through similar religious experiences and brought as strong a message as Fox (Barbour 1988, 25).

More accurately, Fox was the "preeminent figure in the early Quaker movement" (Oliver 2007, xii). Like many in a chaotic decade of war, famine, and depression, Fox wandered restlessly before he was twenty. He argued theology everywhere, and in 1646–1647, a series of religious "openings" came to him as insights that convinced him of the truth of ideas already common among separatists and Baptists (Barbour 1988, 26). For four years, Fox had sought a new way to gain direct access to God.

"When all my hopes in men were gone, so that I had nothing outwardly to help me, nor could I tell what to do, then, O then, I heard a voice which said, 'There is One, even Christ Jesus, that can speak to thy condition.'" And when I heard it, my heart did leap for joy." He developed the idea of the Inner Light within each person (Whalen 1991, 15). He also saw within himself "that there is an ocean of darkness and death, but an infinite ocean of light and love, which flowed over the ocean of darkness" (Barbour 1988, 26–27).

In 1647, he began preaching his new religious ideas and won converts in northern England. Five years later, "he organized the Society of Friends" (Whalen 1991, 15). Pendle Hill is a site in England that has special meaning to Quakers. In 1642, George Fox felt an inward call to climb Pendle Hill to, as in Isaiah 40:9, "Sound forth the day of the Lord . . . The Lord let me see in what places he had a great people to be gathered" (Barbour 1988, 27).

George Fox articulated a desire to remove the causes of war. He refused to join Cromwell's army and stated that he lived in "the virtue of that life and power that took away the occasion of all wars" (Barbour, 27). He spent many years in prison for his beliefs as did many Quakers. They sometimes gained adherents when other prisoners admired their deep commitment to their faith.

Fox and his followers believed that their convictions arose from an experience of the "Light of Christ Within." It was a call to live up to the measure of Light given to each person. It resulted in practical righteousness of each person living out one's faith. Early Quakers believed they were bringing alive the witness of first-century Christians. William Penn, the founder of Pennsylvania, said that Quakerism was "primitive Christianity revived."

The Inner Light

George Fox taught that each person is enlightened by God through the Holy Spirit, described as the Inner Light. Although the Bible was very important to the early Quakers, they felt that the same Spirit, which inspired the Scriptures, could be directly experienced by every person. The Spark of the Divine was "that of God in every person." Their Meeting for Worship was based in silent meditation in which each worshiper could be inspired with a message by the Holy Spirit which could be shared.

The "Quaker tries to live by the Inner Light. The Inner Light is not conscience but it is that which enlightens conscience. Quaker theologians usually describe the Inner Light as 'that of God in each man.' People discern the Inner Light when they silently and patiently wait for God to speak to them. Such direct illumination is far superior to the written revelation of the Bible or Tradition of the church, in the Quaker view" (Whalen 1991, 6).

The Term *Quaker*

Whalen tells how the term *Quaker* came to describe the Society of Friends. George Fox was brought before a magistrate to answer for his radical and unorthodox views. "Fox warned the judge that even he must tremble and quake at the Word of the Lord. The judge asked Fox if he were a 'Quaker.' The name Quaker stuck and is now accepted by Friends," even though meant to be derogatory (Whalen 1991, 3).

The Early Quakers Rejected the Sacraments, Tithes, John Blackburn's Horse

Early Quakers rejected the sacraments and tithing in payment of priests. My earliest known Blackburn ancestor, John Blackburn of Armagh, Ireland, had a horse taken by the local priest in payment of his tithe, even though the practice had been outlawed by the distant Parliament in London.

Barbour also lists rejecting holy days and places, titles, wedding rings, pagan names for months and weekdays, and other medieval superstition by early Friends. In dress and speech, on titles and luxuries, Baptists and Quakers spoke as Puritans with working-class accents. They rejected water Baptism and wine in Communion and the supreme authority of Scripture text (Barbour 1988, 31).

Quaker Worship

A statement distributed at the World Council of Churches meeting in 1948 describes traditional Quaker worship:

> Worship, according to the ancient practice of the Religious Society of Friends, is entirely without human direction or supervision. A group of devout persons come together and sit down quietly with no prearrangement, each seeking to have an immediate sense of divine leading and to know at first hand the presence of the living Christ. It is not wholly accurate to say that such a meeting is held on the basis of silence; it is more accurate to say that it is held on the basis of "holy obedience." (Whalen 1991, 9)

Strict Honesty

Strict honesty was characteristic of Quakers. They "invented the price tag" in contrast to charging "whatever the traffic will bear." Quakers became prominent merchants and bankers because of the trust they gained through their honesty. Cooper refers to "a one price system in merchandising, which reflected their commitment to integrity both in the pricing and in the quality of goods and services offered for sale" (Cooper 2000, 166).

Care of Employees

Quakers employers were known for paying fair wages and caring for the welfare of their staff. "Friends became involved in business, industry, and commerce not just for personal gain but to provide quality goods and services at an equitable price to the consumer and to improve the working and living conditions of the laborers" (Cooper 2000, 130).

Education

The early Quakers wanted their children to get a "guarded education," away from the pernicious materialistic influences of mainstream culture. In America, they established schools when they built meetinghouses on the frontier. Prestigious schools such as Haverford, Swarthmore, Bryn Mawr, Cornell, and Johns Hopkins were established by Quakers. In England Quakers produced prominent scientists, inventors, industrialists, merchants, and bankers. Because they refused to swear oaths, they were denied entry into Cambridge and Oxford. They went to Scotland where the "Scottish Renaissance" had resulted because John Knox wanted all Presbyterians to be able to read the Bible.

American Quakers have produced scientists, writers, and public figures far out of proportion to their numbers. John Greenleaf Whittier was known as the Quaker poet. Susan B. Anthony and Lucretia Mott led the fight for votes for women and equality of the sexes. Dorothea Dix pioneered in the movement to get better treatment for the mentally ill (Whalen 1991, 30).

Simplicity

Simplicity was important to early Quakers. They want to avoid showing off material wealth and to keep life simple in order to be obedient to the leadings of the Inner Light. It was seen in the plain architecture of meetinghouses and plain dress. The girls at Scattergood Friends School were to use makeup sparingly and wear simple outfits.

Quaker Values Are Special Testimonies
(Barbour 1988, 40-46)

"Quaker actions have always expressed as special 'Testimonies' of truthfulness, simplicity, equality and peace." They emerge from the leadings of the Light or Spirit of God (Barbour and Frost, 40–46).

> In that early period there was a testimony against paying tithes to the established church, a testimony against oaths (swearing) in courts of law, a testimony against wars and fighting, a testimony against using titles—to express their concern for equality, a testimony against 'hat honor'—bowing before superiors. There were testimonies about 'plain' language and dress and about simplicity in the furnishing of Quaker homes. These and other testimonies gave expression to the burning issues of the day. (Cooper 2000, 130–131)

As people who were each led by their experience of an Inner Light, early Friends were careful to examine personal motives. Friends always looked twice at "unexpected impulses in case self-will or pleasure were their source." They expected the Light of Truth to be consistent, and its leadings, though individualized, to be recognizably similar for all times and persons, including biblical prophets, apostles, and all Friends. What one Quaker felt as a leading was tested against guidance from the Bible, and after 1656, submitted to the joint guidance given to a group by the Spirit as the "Sense of the Meeting." Each of the norms that early Friends accepted were considered to be Truth.

This standard applied, for example, to honesty in the marketplace but also to the plain language as true grammar (Barbour 1988, 40).

When George Fox dictated his Journal, he summarized Quaker ethics: He was "Called to turn people from darkness to the light that they might receive Christ Jesus; to bring them away from all ceremonies and churches; to use *thee* and *thou*; to refuse to take off their hats to anyone; to cry for justice to judges; to warn against drink, sports, May games, vanities and cheating; and to reject oaths" (Barbour 1988, 41). Modern Friends include these testimonies within concerns for honesty, equality, simplicity, and peace (Barbour 1988, 40–41).

1

Truthfulness and Honesty

ONE OF THE REASONS Quaker merchants were especially successful was their reputation for truthfulness. Quakers are reputed to be the inventors of the price tag during a time when it was customary to ask a price according to what the merchant thought they could get.

I learned in grade school to curb my Quaker honesty when a teacher told me not to tell on another to assign guilt. Even though our parents taught us Quaker truthfulness, there it was out of order. Little white lies are good. My wife likes fogging to keep interpersonal harmony.

Quakers rejected oaths as contrary to Jesus teaching: "Let your yea be yea, and your nay be nay" and "Swear not at all, neither by the Heavens for that is God's throne, nor by the Earth, as that is God's footstool" (Matt. 5:33–37). Even today, people in America are allowed to affirm instead of swear an oath in court.

The commitment of English Friends to honesty led to stunning achievements in industry, management, science, and commerce. The idea that those barred from political power (for refusal to swear oaths) and subjected to serious discrimination will channel their creative efforts elsewhere is borne out by eighteenth-century Quakers. Plain living, dependable work habits, and inventiveness made them prosperous. Intermarriage among Quaker families meant that the capital accumulated by one generation was passed on. By the mid-eighteenth century English Quakers had become almost a clan of extended kinfolk bound together by patterns of commerce and religion (Barbour 1988, 86).

A story is told about two boys who vowed to catch a prominent member of their Meeting in an untruth. One knocked on the door and was invited in. A minute later, the other knocked. Meanwhile, the first boy climbed out a window. When the second boy asked, "Is John here?" he expected this Friend to answer untruthfully, "Yes." Instead, the "weighty" Friend replied, about the parlor, "I left him there a minute ago." They all had a good laugh.

2

Equality

EARLY FRIENDS UPHELD THE statement of Jesus to "call no man Master" to support equality. They came from regions in England that valued independence and status equality. The plain language was a refusal to use titles and gestures of honor to humble everyone equally, rather than honoring everyone with the "royal *you*."

Equality applied to God's ability to speak through any receptive person. The equality in ministry of all Friends, rich and poor, young and old, educated and unschooled, and especially women and men, was noticed by everyone in the 1650s. They pointed out that Jesus and his disciples were workingmen. They also stood out in their faith in non-Christian cultures, assuming that God's Spirit worked through Turks, Chinese, or American Indians (Barbour 1988, 43).

A story on TV told of a slave freed by Quakers who addressed James Madison as James. Because his wife, Dolley Madison, was raised as a Quaker, that form of address did not offend him.

Quakers were very active in helping runaway slaves in the nineteenth century and operated the Underground Railroad. Slaves would go to southern Pennsylvania where they knew they could get help if they heard *thee* and *thou* used by Quaker farmers.

3

Quaker Simplicity

UNTIL ABOUT 1850, QUAKERS used distinctively
plain meetinghouses, homes, and clothing to cut
down human pride and distractions (Barbour 1988,
4).

Quaker simplicity in clothes and the plain
architecture of meetinghouses were well-known in
America. Even substantial stone structures had simple outlines. In photographs of early Scattergood
Friends School students, almost all wore black, with
a few in brown or grey (Berquist book). When I was
at Scattergood Friends School, the girls used simple makeup. We were required, however, to dress up
for Saturday supper. Even in the twentieth century,
some Ohio Conservative Friends used snaps rather
than buttons.

Friends rejected pagan names for days the week.
Wednesday for Woden's Day became "Fourth Day,"

and Mars's (god of war) month, March, became "Third Month" as a rejection of pagan violence (Barbour 1988, 42).

4

The Plain Language

THE PLAIN LANGUAGE (*THEE* and *thy* instead of *you* and *yours*) was used by early Friends. It is honesty in the grammatically correct use of language to address another individual as *thee* and *thou* instead of *you*. You correctly refers to more than one person (plural grammatically). The usage of *you* developed in England as a form of special respect and honor, the "royal *you*." Even today in Spanish and French, the second person, or *thee*, is used for family members, children, and people of lower status.

The plain language is still in use in some families. I use *thee* and *thy* with siblings, cousins, and Scattergood Friends School schoolmates with whom I have exchanged annual letters for over fifty years. In West Branch, Iowa, a cousin, Jessie Blackburn Jones, who ran a Dry Goods Store, was renowned for always addressing her customers in the plain language.

Many early Quakers spent time in prison for failing to swear oaths of allegiance to the crown, join the armed forces, address the magistrates properly, or remove their hats in deference to their superiors.

The use of the plain language was widespread even beyond Ohio and Iowa Wilburite Quakers, even into the 1970s. While waiting for Meeting for Worship to start at the Sandy Spring Friends Meeting in Maryland, I overheard a young person criticize another: "*Thee* is an obscenity." A Quaker was talking with a farmer using the plain language.

When the farmer seemed puzzled, the Quaker explained: "*Thee* sees. We use the plain language."

The farmer replied, "You'll have to talk plainer than that, buddy, if you want me to understand you."

The 1903 Catalogue of Scattergood Friends School states, "While the aim of the school is to give a substantial English education, suited to fit the average person for the ordinary duties of life, and at the same time prepare students for higher institutions of learning, yet it is still its distinctive purpose to shield the young from hurtful temptations and distracting tendencies during the character-forming period." The students are expected to be "consistent in dress and are to use the pain language in accordance with the well-known testimony of Friends upon these subjects and are to be affable and courteous in their intercourse with all." (Berquist 1990, 13)

In November 1986, Laurence Barclay DeWees gave an account of his memories of Scattergood Friends School: "I recently ran across one of my old report cards . . . I noticed one item: 'Deportment satisfactory, except occasional improper use of the plural language.' That was bordering on profanity in those days. I love the old 'thee' language, and now no one ever uses it, even in Quaker meetings. I am pretty sure that no one at Scattergood uses it, or knows what it meant. I still use it while visiting with old friends. It always seemed so simple, and so friendly." (Berquist 1990, 27)

We Blackburn siblings always used the plain language. My wife, Willa Bruce, overheard me talking with my mother on the phone, and ever since, we have used the plain language with each other. When my mother first met Willa, she asked, in her own inimitable and original usage, "Is this a '*thee*' person?" I use it with my First, Second, and even Third cousins. I had five Second Cousins at Scattergood.

5

The Peace Testimony

THE PEACE TESTIMONY HAS been an essential element of Quakerism from the very founding of the Society of Friends in the seventeenth century. Their first corporate statement, addressed to English King Charles II in 1661, included, "We do testify to the world that the Spirit of Christ which leads us into all truth, will never move us to fight and war against any man with outward weapons, neither for the Kingdom of Christ nor for the kingdoms of this world" (Cooper 2000, 135).

Quakers sometimes quoted the Gospel of John: "My kingship is not of this world; if my kingship were of this world, my servants would fight, that I might not be handed over to the Jews; but my kingship is not from this world" (John 18:36).

Quakers treasure The New Testament. They take seriously the admonition of Jesus to "love your enemies" and His statement "Blessed are the peace-makers." They feel that the way of the cross of Jesus is entirely inconsistent with war or preparation for war.

Paul wrote, "See that none of you repays evil with evil, but always seek to do good to one another and to all" (Thess. 5:15).

Isaiah prophesies, "And they shall beat their swords into plowshares, and their spears into pruning hooks; nation shall not lift up sword against nations, neither shall they learn war anymore" (Isa. 2:4).

Jesus taught, "But I say to you, Love your enemies and pray for those who persecute you, so that you may be sons of your Father who is in heaven; for he makes his sun rise on the evil and on the good, and sends rain on the just and on the unjust" (Matt. 5:44). And "But I say to you that hear, Love your enemies, do good to those who hate you, pray for those who abuse you" (Luke 6:27–28).

Paul wrote, "Beloved, never avenge yourselves, but leave it to the wrath of God; for it is written, 'Vengeance is mine, I will repay, says the Lord'" (Rom. 12:19).

Quakers are recognized the world over for their peace witness. The Society of Friends received the Nobel Peace Prize in 1947, jointly awarded to the

American Friends Service Committee and Friends' Service Council of England. Quakers are among the Historic Peace Churches, including the Mennonites and Church of the Brethren.

A story is told about a Quaker who heard a burglar downstairs. The Quaker grabbed a shotgun he had been keeping for a friend. He went down and confronted the burglar: "Friend, I would not for the world harm thee, but thee is standing where I am about to shoot."

Two iconic Americans explain their objections to war: "Never think that war, no matter how necessary, nor how justified, is not a crime (Ernest Hemingway 1899–1961). And "I hate war as only a soldier who has lived it can, only as one who has seen its brutality, its futility, its stupidity" (Dwight D. Eisenhower 1890–1969.)

Section 2

Wilburites

THE QUAKERS IN IOWA who founded Scattergood Friends School were Wilburites. They still maintain the silent meditation of the traditional Quaker Meeting for Worship in which they wait for an inspirational message from God, or the Holy Spirit, which can then be shared with the other worshippers. This was the pattern which the Quakers brought over from England to America, especially in the Quaker Colony of Pennsylvania founded by William Penn.

In twenty-first century America, it is the Wilburite Conservative Friends who have most consistently championed the "ancient testimonies and doctrines of Friends" (Cooper 2000, 43).

The Wilburite Quakers

Both of my parents were from a branch of the Quakers called the Wilburites. Daddy was from Ohio Yearly Meeting and Mother from Iowa Yearly Meeting. I believe they met at Olney Friends School in Barnesville, Ohio. I found in a listing of Olney alumnae that they both attended Olney. Mother also attended one or more years at Scattergood Friends School and Westtown, a very prestigious Quaker school near Philadelphia. She told me that the headmaster, a cousin, seemed to look down on her, maybe because of her Iowa accent, and perhaps also for her clothing, which probably was more plain than many of her schoolmates from Philadelphia. Perhaps also she was more plain, direct, and sincere than many of her more citified schoolmates.

When I visited Scattergood in June 2014, I was pleased to find that the Iowa Yearly Meeting still provides guidance to Scattergood School. When I attended Scattergood in the 1950s, local meetings had many members who were farmers. William Penn Young, my grandfather, was a prosperous farmer near Whittier, Iowa.

Barbour and Frost (1988) mentions Scattergood: "Whose community spirit, shared work, and teaching have drawn many students from other branches of Quakerism" (Barbour 1988, 233).

There are still active Wilburite Quaker meetings in Iowa and Ohio.

Iowa Wilburite Friends Want to Preserve Ancient Quakerism

I did not appreciate how distinctive my Wilburite heritage was until long after I had graduated from Scattergood Friends School.

From the very beginning of the Society of Friends, the values of Quakers have been in stark contrast to the predominant values of society, or the world. Jesus once said, "My kingdom is not of this world" (John 18:36). "Propelled by the pioneering spirit and an aversion to slavery, Friends from eastern and southeastern states began during the nineteenth century to move into the Northwest Territory beyond the Ohio River. By 1835 the first Quaker settlement in Iowa was staked out at Salem, which became the hub of an area sprinkled with numerous Friends meetings. Later, some families who had first settled in Ohio and Indiana moved on to Cedar County, Iowa and by 1849, they were holding meeting for worship in homes" (Berquist 1990, 1). "It was only a few Friends who really founded in 1854 or 1855 the Hickory Grove Meeting," next to Scattergood (Berquist 1990, 2). My mother was from Springville, Iowa, near Whittier, in Linn County.

In *Scattergood Friends School 1890–1990*, Carolyn Treadway writes, "The unique character of this small group of Wilburite Friends is not easy to explain. Among the things which distinguished these Friends were simple, unadorned clothing and their mode of worship, in which the silent communion was broken only when an individual felt led by the Spirit to speak (Berquist 1990, 2–3).

According to Whalen, "A conservative group called the Wilburites separated themselves in 1845". (Whalen 1991, 25) A Wilburite is a follower of John Wilbur, an Orthodox quietist Quaker who emphasized the need to give primary attention to the "Inward Christ." In his journal, he warned against "running ahead of the Guide" (Berquist 1990, 2). Quietism stressed the complete subordination of self-will in the meeting for worship and in daily life (Berquist 1990, 6–7). Conservative Quakerism "believed it had preserved the form and spirit of ancient Quakerism" (Taber 1976, 72)

Punshon explains,

Though John Wilbur's views did not obtain a large following, or express widely held sentiments, they did prove capable of sustaining a small but permanently influential group now known as Conservative Friends. There are three Conservative Yearly Meetings—Iowa, North Carolina and Ohio—and they are an important part of the Quaker landscape. In the past, they survived because they rejected many of the Gurneyite innovations and drew together in close groups to maintain what they saw as the true traditions of the Society. (Punshon 1984, 198)

There are three Conservative Yearly Meetings— Iowa, North Carolina and Ohio—and they are an important part of the Quaker landscape. "In the past, they survived because they rejected many of the Gurneyite innovations and drew together in close groups to maintain what they saw as the true traditions of the Society" (Punshon 1984, 198).

I was struck recently by a TV story about the Dark Ages. During these centuries in Europe, the monasteries were a beacon of culture and light. A commentator noted that maintaining strict silence was a means to curb the ego of the individual monks.

"Wilburite" conservatives in New England, Philadelphia, Ohio, Indiana (and Iowa) kept their isolation from the wider culture and in dress, in their schools, and at home kept many Quaker customs into the twentieth century (Barbour 1988, 8). They had drawn apart from the "larger body" because of changes resulting from the influence of Joseph John Gurney and the Great Revival.

Before the end of the century, they became associated with other Friends, called Conservatives, who, for similar reasons, had withdrawn from other Quaker bodies in order to preserve the beliefs and practices that they most cherished (Berquist 1990, 2–3). Characteristic testimonies were simplicity, honesty, temperance in all things, peace as opposed to war, and human equality (Berquist 1990, x). Whalen writes that "about 1,800 Conservative Friends continue the Wilburite tradition" (Whalen 1991, 26).

Some Characteristics of Quakers, Especially of Wilburites

The Wilburite Quakers may be the most traditional of any Quakers in the twenty-first century

Society of Friends. Whalen (1991) lists characteristics of Quakers that apply especially to Wilburite Friends:

1. **Social Concerns**. Strong commitment to social concerns including peace, racial equality, prison reform, abolition of capital punishment, slum clearance, support of the United Nations, coexistence with Communist states, mental health programs, and freedom of conscience and of religion (Whalen 1991, 30).

   William Penn said, "True godliness does not turn men out of the world but enables them to live better in it, and excites their endeavors to mend it" (Whalen 1991, 31). The Nobel Peace Prize was awarded jointly to the American Friends Service Committee (AFSC) and its British counterpart, the Friends Service Council, in 1947 (Whalen 1991, 4). While the Wilburites are conservative in maintaining traditions from the earliest days of Quakerism, they are very liberal on social and political issues.

   Melinda Lilly, in *Quakers in Early America* (2003) writes that William Penn in 1681 convinced the king of England to give him the land that became Pennsylvania. The Quakers thought all people had a right to their beliefs, and they lived in peace with the Native Americans. Penn even engaged in friendly foot races with these neighbors.

In 1701, William Penn wrote the Charter of Privileges based on Quaker ideas of freedom, and this helped lead to the US Constitution. Fifty years later, the Liberty Bell was made, and it honored the Charter of Privileges, which protected the religious freedom of the people of Pennsylvania and granted some governmental power to its Assembly (Lilly).

"The Quakers not only developed Pennsylvania and New Jersey but at one time controlled Rhode Island, Delaware, and North Carolina. By 1700, according to Quaker historian, Elbert Russell, 'Friends were the greatest single religious organiza-tion in the English colonies as a whole, both in their influence and in their promise'" (Russell, *The History of Quakerism*, 124, in Whalen 1991, 22).

Cooper comments, "When one makes even a cursory review of the history of Friends' involvement and work in philanthropic, peace and social concerns, one must stand amazed at the incredible extent to which a group so small numerically has been involved in ministering to the ills and needs of the world. The list is both impressive and far-reaching: education, prison reform, religious freedom, abolition of slavery, Indian work, care of the poor and the insane, capital punishment, temperance, war and famine relief, peace and service work, women's rights, economic and racial justice, ecological concerns, and the list goes on and on. Also, Friends became involved in business, industry, and commerce not just for personal gain but to provide quality goods and services at an equitable price to the consumer and to improve the working and living conditions of the laborers. The history of Quaker philanthropy is an exhilarating story." (Cooper 2000, 130). [Lucretia Mott, a leader in women' suffrage, was married to a distant cousin—my grandmother was Mary Mott Young. Wilmer Cooper is a cousin on the Blackburn side of my family.]

2. **Silent Worship.** The Wilburites had silent worship, with no set prayers, no sermon, no alter, and no set scripture readings or hymns.

3. **No Sacred Days.** They had no sacred days or places, although First Day, or Sunday, was a regular day for worship and a day of rest. They did not make much of a fuss over Christmas, Easter, or other holy days.

4. **Consensus Decisions.** They did not make decisions by majority rule but instead by consensus. The book *Beyond Majority Rule* was written by a Jesuit who explains how consensus decision-making works in Quaker meetings for business: the Presiding Clerk obtains a sense of the meeting, which means unity but not necessarily unanimity.

5. **Women Equal with Men.** Women hold equal power with men (Whalen 1991, 11–12). Iowa and Ohio meetinghouses had separate sides for men and women, which could be completely closed off. Following the school year 1917–1918, Scattergood was almost closed due to resistance to spending $5,000 on constructing a boys' dormitory, which some thought would change the character of the school, with my grandfather, William Penn Young, serving as clerk.

   When the women's meeting received the clerk's minute, an earnest and unanimous protest against the action of the men's meeting was entered. After pleading with them to rescind their action, they were so far successful to get their consent to proceed with the work without leaving the Hickory Grove Quarterly Meeting in debt (Berquist 1990, 36–37). Thus, Scattergood School, which has meant so much to Iowa Wilburite Quakers and the Blackburn family could have gone out of existence under the leadership of our grandfather Young.

I have wonderful memories of getting a coal fire started in the little pot-bellied stove in the Hickory Grove meetinghouse early on a cold First Day morning, when I was on Buildings and Grounds crew, to have the men's side of the meetinghouse warm for Meeting for Worship.

As students, we did not sort ourselves by gender but spread ourselves along the benches without any thought of the gender of the person sitting next to us (at least, that was the theory, but everyone knows us teenage boys would try to sit next to a girl if we could do it without being too obvious).

6. **Simple Clothing.** In clothing, they wore no fancy dress. The boys usually wore black or brown, and the girls, black, gray, or white

dresses without a lot of frills. In photographs of early students in the Scattergood book, however, I see Iowa Quakers wearing a lot of frills and neckties (Berquist). I believe that Iowa Wilburite Friends were substantially less conservative and traditional than Ohio Wilburite Friends. I was a birthright member of both Ohio and Iowa Yearly Meetings because my father was a member in Ohio and my mother a member in Iowa.

Before Scattergood was started in 1890, Iowa students got a reduction in tuition of $15 in the winter and $10 in the summer to compensate for travel costs to attend Olney Friends School in Barnesville, Ohio. I believe my parents met at Olney as I found in a directory that they had graduated only two or three years apart. Several of my Blackburn and Young relatives attended Olney Friends School before Scattergood opened, including Wilmer A. Cooper, a third cousin who was the founding dean of the Earlham School of Religion, and my first cousin, Charlotte Carpenter.

In a photo of a wedding in which my mother, Lorena, at age four sits on my grandmother's lap (Mary Mott Young), I noted a lot of very fancy clothing. Iowa farmers benefitted financially from the opening of rich Midwestern agriculture to the demand for crops back east and abroad. The development of railroads must have been a key factor. My grandfather, William Penn Young, was a prosperous farmer near Whittier, Iowa, who sent my mother to Westtown School, a very prestigious Quaker school near Philadelphia. Her cousin was headmaster. She used to speak disparagingly of him. I suspect he looked down his nose at her for her rural Iowa Quaker dress and manners.

My mother also went to Scattergood where her older sister, Florence, was a teacher. I did not realize this until I read this in the Scattergood book, although my mother must have told me (Berquist 1990, 29). Midwest prairie farmland was richer and cheaper than land in New England and Pennsylvania. Quakers moved and settled in cohesive groups and migrants kept their affiliations with home Meetings and new Monthly and Yearly Meetings were formed. Quaker primary and secondary schools were linked to each Meeting (Barbour 1988, 8). In 1958 when I worked at Olney Friends

School, there were still Friends who wore very plain and dark clothing, including jackets which buttoned all the way up to their chins. They never wore neckties to Meeting for Worship.

7. **Plain Meetinghouses.** Their meetinghouses had very plain lines with no fancy adornments and no steeples. They separated the genders, with one side for men and the other for women, but at Scattergood, we all sat mixed on the men's side. I have no recollection of how we chose where to sit for Meeting for Worship, but probably with our classmates and friends—it did not really matter because we would sit silently and not whisper to each other.

At a gathering of former Young Friends of North America from all over the country and the world, at Olney, in about 2007, I observed that at one meeting all the attendees sat up near the front, in stark contrast to the behavior of most churches I have seen where most prefer to sit in or near the back.

8. **The Plain Language.** They used the plain language, the use of *thee* and *thou* instead of *you*. This is now mostly abandoned except in my Blackburn family and by me with my

Scattergood friends and cousins. Eric Curtis, Dean of Students at Earlham College in the 1950s, had a pronounced British accent and a degree from Oxford. He used *thou* in a way I had never heard before, like "Art thou going?" This was in contrast to "Is thee going?" which was the usage I grew up with. I think it was because many of my Wilburite ancestors were from rural areas and were not highly educated.

Barbour writes that "American Quakers who say 'Is thee going?' preserve old rural English with Norse verb forms and are closer to early moorland Quaker language than English Friends who ask "Art thou going?" (Barbour 1988, 47). This usage of *thou*, while probably more grammatically correct than the use of *thee*, which I grew up with, would sound strange to my siblings.

9. **No Clergy.** The Meetings for Worship had no pastors or ministers to give sermons, but instead all waited in reverent silence for any message that might be provided to the worshipers by the Inner Light, Holy Spirit, or God. One of my cousins, Wilmer Cooper, wrote a charming little book, *Growing Up Plain*, in which he explains that he concealed

from his father that he had been ordained because as an Ohio Wilburite Quaker, his father would have not approved. Wilmer was the founding Dean of the Earlham School of Religion.

10. **Queries.** "At least once a year each Monthly Meeting makes what amounts to a group examination of conscience. The members of the congregation answer a series of questions or queries, posed by the Yearly Meeting, which relate to the spiritual state of the meeting." (Whalen 1991, 12).

   Barbour (109) quotes twelve queries from 1743, which show the deep spirituality of eighteenth-century Friends. The vivid, colorful, and startling expressions show the language and customs of that time:

1. Are Friends careful to attend Meetings at the time appointed and to refrain from sleeping or chewing tobacco in Meetings?
2. Do Friends stay clear of excess in 'drinking Drams'?
3. Do young Friends keep company for marriage with non-Friends or marry without parental consent?

4. Are Friends clear from tattling, tale bearing, and meddling.
5. Do Friends stay free from music houses, dancing, and gambling?
6. Are Friends careful 'to train up their Children in the Nurture and Fear of the Lord, and to restrain them from vice and Evil Company, and keep them to plainness of Speech and Apparel'?
7. Are the poor taken care of, are their children put to school and then apprenticed out to Friends, and do Friends apprentice their children only to Friends?
8. Are Friends cautious not to launch into business beyond what they can do?
9. Are Friends careful not to remove without a certificate?
10. Are Friends on guard not to deprive the king of his duties?
11. Do Friends stay clear of the importing or buying of Negroes?
12. Are Friends prudent in settling their affairs and in leaving wills? (Barbour 1988, 109)

A flavor of the queries in the twenty-first century is seen in a leaflet: "Advices and Queries of Ohio Yearly Meeting of the Religious Society of Friends." The first query is typical: "Are meetings for worship well and punctually attended? Is our behavior therein conducive to meditation and communion with God? Do we maintain a waiting, spiritual worship and a free gospel ministry? Do we welcome others to share this fellowship?"

The second query asks, "Do we cherish a forgiving spirit, and strive to 'walk in love, as Christ also hath loved us'? Is each one of us careful for the reputation of others? Are we ever mindful to love our neighbor as ourselves? If differences threaten to disrupt the Christian harmony between the members, is prompt action taken?"

These queries are familiar because I heard them in my youth and when I attended Scattergood Friends School. They show the deep spirituality of my Wilburite ancestors. When I was active in the 1960s in the Quaker Meeting in Columbus, Ohio, which my parents had helped to found, I can remember being very surprised and a little bit annoyed at one family who were always late to Meeting.

I found the following in a 1950 "Newsletter of the North Columbus Friends Meeting," which Daddy had sent to us at Scattergood. It shows a continuity with the rich spiritual heritage from the sixteenth century.

"Query for November. At the October monthly meeting someone suggested that The Query to be read at the next monthly meeting be printed in THE NEWSLETTER, so Friends might be meditating upon it before meeting. The November Query is:

"2. Ministry: Is the vocal ministry in your meeting exercised under the direct leading of the Holy Spirit, without prearrangement and in the simplicity and sincerity of Truth? Do you foster the use and growth of the spiritual gifts of your members?"

11. **No clergy for weddings.** Weddings among the Wilburites are conducted with the two members of the couple repeating their vows to each other, which are often written by the couple themselves. This is also the custom of many other Quaker congregations beside the Wilburites. At one time, wedding rings were not used by Friends (Barbour 1988,

31), but that custom probably disappeared for most Quakers before the twentieth century. The couple have to obtain the consent of the Meeting to marry under the care of the Meeting.

In the ceremony, each declares, "In the presence of the Lord and of these our friends, I take thee, to be my wife (or husband), promising with divine assistance to be unto thee a loving and faithful husband (or wife) so long as we both shall live."

I have heard this <u>exact</u> wording in at least three marriage ceremonies. Then, all of those present sign the marriage certificate as witnesses (Whalen, 12). My brother, William J. Blackburn III, was married to his Jewish-heritage wife, Doris Seidel, in the Florida Avenue meetinghouse in Washington, DC where Herbert Hoover, who was born in West Branch, Iowa (two miles from Scattergood) attended.

I came across in my archives a copy of the Marriage Certificate of my parents, handwritten on high-quality parchment about 8 inches by 6 inches, as follows:

In large hand printed words: "Whereas." Next in large print, with bold and large W:

William J. Blackburn Jr."; Next in smaller letters, cursive: "of Salem, in the County of Columbiana, in the state of Ohio, son of William J. and Elizabeth C. Blackburn and"— Next in large print, with bold and large L: "Lorena Young." Next in smaller letters, cursive: "of Whittier, in the county of Linn, in the state of Iowa, daughter of William P. (for Penn), and Mary M. (for Mott) Young, having made known their intentions of marriage to each other, [Next Page] in cursive: "in a Monthly Meeting of the Religious Society of Friends, held at Whittier, Iowa, and, having the consent of their parents, their proposals were allowed by the meeting. These are to certify, that, for the full accomplishment of their intentions, this twenty-fifth day of the First Month, in the year of our Lord one-thousand nine hundred and thirty, they appeared in a public meeting of Friends, held at Whittier, Iowa, and publicly declared that, in the presence of the Lord, they took each other for husband and wife, promising, with divine assistance, to be loving and faithful companions until death should separate them.

"And, as a further confirmation thereof, they did then and there to these presents subscribe their names – she according to the custom of marriage, adopting the name of her husband,

William J. Blackburn Jr.
LORENA Young Blackburn

"And we, whose names are hereunto affixed, being present at the solemnization, have as witnesses thereto subscribed our names:

(There follows, not in alphabetical order, several close relatives, including Lorena's sister and brother, and the two children of Lorena's sister. Lorena's parents, William P.(for Penn) Young and Mary M. (Mott) Young, were the fourteenth and fifteenth signatures. There were a total of 73 signatures, with ten Mott signatures, and many others which I recognize as first or second cousins. I recognize many other names of people who were relatives of fellow students at Scattergood and who were prominent members of Iowa Yearly Meeting. The only Blackburn cousins I was sure of were William's first cousin, Ruth H. Blackburn, and another cousin, Jesse B. (Blackburn) Jones, who must have been a third cousin. She was famous with her dry goods store in West Branch, Iowa, near the birthplace of Quaker, Herbert Hoover, because she always addressed every customer with the plain language of "thee" rather than "you."

[In a tiny hand at the bottom of page 5] "Recorded as Pages 50 and 51 in Book 2 of marriage certificates, Springville Monthly Meeting of Friends, by Wm. P. Bedell."

12. **No Baptism or Communion.** The sacraments of Baptism and the Lord's Supper (communion) were rejected. They reasoned that no rites or ritual were needed to discern the Inner Light (Whalen 1991, 13).

13. **William Penn Statement.** They agreed with William Penn: "I abhor two principles in religion and pity them that own them . . . The first is obedience to authority without conviction; and the other is destroying them that differ from me for God's sake" (Whalen 1991, 21).

14. **Quietism.** Quietism was pervasive. After the American Revolution, Quakerism began to harden into a peculiar system. Abraham Lincoln described his Quaker ancestors as peculiar people. The doctrine of Quietism, which was an emphasis upon being attentive to the Inner Light, stifled missionary activities in England and infected American Quakers as well. Any Friend who married outside the Quaker community was read out of meeting, that is, disowned or

removed from formal membership. I have in my notes, based from the conversation I had with an Iowa Quaker, a story of a member who "was put out of Meeting" (Margaret Hoge).

Art, music, games, dances, the theater, and other pastimes were forbidden. The money spent on frills could be used for good works (Whalen 1991, 23). I heard a story when I was a student at Cornell University that Ezra Cornell was asked to admit that he had made a mistake for marrying a non-Friend, but he replied that it was the best decision he had ever made. This kind of narrow inward-oriented concern for purity kept the Society of Friends from attracting new members.

15. **No Fiction.** Fiction was forbidden. At one time, fiction was considered by Quakers to be inappropriate and frivolous for Friends. Probably this has not been true since the nineteenth century or early in the twentieth century as we at Scattergood were encouraged to read the classical works of fiction. I personally have always been less interested in fiction than non-fiction, but I remember

greatly enjoying *Pride and Prejudice, Jane Eyre, A Tale of Two Cities*, and *Scottish Chiefs*.

16. **Simple Calendar.** Pagan names were not used in the calendar. The conventional names of the days of the week were taken from pagan forms, so the Quakers used the terms "First Day" and "Second Day" instead. The origin of March is in Mars (god of war), and Wednesday is in "Woden's Day," which reflects pagan violence (Barbour 1988, 42). This practice has probably been almost totally abandoned in the twenty-first century. In the letters we received from our parents in 1950, they referred to Second Day instead of Tuesday and Third Month instead of March.

17. **No Oaths.** Friends refuse to swear oaths. The admonition of Jesus "Swear not at all" is from Matthew 5:34. Today an affirmation is a legal substitute for an oath. In England, in earlier times, the Quakers "suffered in the courts of law or turned down possible political careers" due to this refusal. They could not attend university or serve in Parliament. They could, however, attend university in Scotland, where many were trained, including many very distinguished scientists and

physicians, even some who made major scientific discoveries. John Dalton became the most important Quaker scientist for his discovery of the law of chemical combinations and calculations of the atomic weights of various elements (Barbour 1988, 87). This refusal avoided a double standard about honesty—one in court "under oath" and another in daily life (Whalen 1991, 24).

18. **Plain Dress.** In the nineteenth century, "colors were forbidden in clothing; the men wore black and the women gray. The suits lacked lapels and extra buttons and were worn without neckties" (Whalen 1991, 23–24). In *Scattergood Friends School 1890–1990* (Berquist), photographs from the late nineteenth and the twentieth century, however, show pictures of boys wearing ties and the girls in very frilly white dresses. I believe Iowa Wilburite Friends were not nearly as conservative as those in Ohio. My mother was from the Iowa group and my father from the Ohio group, but my father was not at all conservative like some of our Ohio relatives.

19. **Avoid Liquor and Gambling.** "A Quaker will avoid liquor and gambling as well as refuse to swear an oath in court; but now-

adays an affirmation is all that is required from those who have a religious objection to oaths" (Whalen 1991, 29).

20. **No Secret Societies.** "Quakers will not join secret societies, such as Freemasonry, which specialize in oaths" (Whalen 1991, 29–30).

Section 3

The Quaker Values and Way of Life of the Blackburn Family

I GREW UP IN a middle-class family in the middle of America in the middle of the twentieth century. My family was typical of families with a father who was a college professor and a mother who stayed home. We were much different from our schoolmates at University School, however, in our Quaker faith.

Two core values of Quakers are their stand against war, as taught by Jesus in the New Testament, and their belief in "that of God in every person." They believed that each human being has access to God through the Inner Light, a light that "enlightens every person in the world." The way of life of the Blackburns flowed from these two values.

1

Be Attuned to The Inner Light

QUAKERS BELIEVE IN "THAT of God in every man (person)." A Scripture which is a basis is John 1:9, which says, "He was the true light that enlightens everyone coming into the world." (Holy Bible, New Revised Standard Version, NY.: Oxford University Press, 1989)

The idea of Quakers that there is "that of God" within each person, leads naturally to the concept of "The Inner Light." Quakers think that each person is able to get divine guidance by being attentive to this "Light". In their traditional silent worship, each individual may get a message to share with the congregation.

Congressman John Lewis talked of "The spark of the divine" in those who were beating him severely. He may have gotten the concept from Dr.

Martin Luther King, who was convinced to use nonviolence by Bayard Rustin, a Quaker.

We children grew up attending traditional Quaker Meeting for Worship based upon silent meditation. We had no Sunday school. When a person had a message to share, they would stand up. The message was seen as inspired by the Inner Light. We accepted this form of worship without question, even without any formal indoctrination. The early Quakers called it "Waiting upon the Lord."

A vivid memory is of a man burning part of a dollar bill in Meeting for Worship. I've forgotten the message, but it must have been about using our resources in accord with our Quaker beliefs.

This attention to inner experience leads to helping to make the world a better place. Quakers put the teachings of Jesus on "Love" at the forefront of their beliefs. They feel that the teachings about loving your neighbor should be a top priority – the very heart of the message of Jesus.

Quakers read the Bible— my grandmother Mary Mott Young in Whittier, Iowa, always started the day with reading the Bible and a period of silent meditation. In Quaker boarding school, we took classes on The Old Testament, the Prophets, the Letters of Paul, and the Gospels as well as The History of

Quakerism. At Quaker Earlham College, I took a course on the Bible and one on World Religions. Deeply religious scholars taught our courses. Hugh Barbour was an internationally recognized authority on The Quakers. In World Religions, taught by Paul Lacey, we explored especially the rich legacy of Hindu and Buddhist texts.

In weekly silent Meetings for Worship, we gained insights and inspiration from fellow worshippers. We taught each other by sharing ideas from our studies of religious teachings. At Scattergood Friends School, faculty shared in Collection the ideas of great leaders in Christianity. We had a rich banquet of knowledge from which to form our individual faith.

The early Quakers developed corporate bodies, like the Monthly Meetings for Business of each Quaker congregation. In their Meeting for Sufferings, they kept track of members who were in prison for their beliefs and helped their families to survive while their breadwinners were suffering for their faith. Corporate bodies were a moderating influence on individual Quakers who might otherwise go off on tangents of strange beliefs not rooted in the biblical heritage of Quakers. The early Quakers were prolific writers of religious tracts. Robert Barclay (1644–1690) wrote a famous classic of theology, *Apology for the True Christian Divinity*, a framework for Quaker faith and practice. Books entitled *Faith and Practice* were produced by Quaker bodies to guide congregations and individuals.

Quakers traditionally did not hand down strict theological teaching nor a system of beliefs. Being attuned to the Inner Light means that each of us develops our own personal faith, with inspiration from the Holy Scriptures and Quakerism. We are also each attentive to the wisdom in the weekly vocal ministry of the Meeting for Worship. I once embarrassed myself in vocal ministry by talking about a godless country. Another member then spoke to suggest that my statement was not appropriate. I recognized that I had made a mistake. It was a good lesson for me on being more thoughtful about my Quaker heritage. Debating another person who has shared in vocal ministry is not considered good form, but in this instance, I am glad I was called to task.

I believe that George Fox, for the Quakers, and John Wesley, for the Methodists, developed foundations for the continuation of each faith by setting up corporate bodies that guided each congregation. The Quakers had Monthly Meetings for Business, which were the governing bodies for each congregation. Larger bodies such as the Yearly Meetings met annually to share their faith and fellowship. Some annual bodies had Quarterly Meetings, which met when Queries were directed to each congregation for self-examination.

2

Promote Peace and Be Active
to Improve the World

THE PEACE TESTIMONY HAS been an essential part of Quakerism from the very founding. Their first corporate statement, addressed to English King Charles II in 1661, stated, "We do testify to the world that the Spirit of Christ which leads us into all truth, will never move us to fight and war against any man with outward weapons, neither for the Kingdom of Christ nor for the kingdoms of this world." (Cooper 2000, 20).

Quakers were diligent in the search for world peace. The Nobel Peace Prize was jointly awarded to the American Friends Service Committee (AFSC) and the Friends' Service Council of England in 1947. Quakers are among the Historic Peace Churches, including the Mennonites and Church of the Brethren.

In America, the Quakers suffered much for their opposition to war and refusal to fight in the American Revolution, although several prominent generals abandoned their Quaker pacifism. One of George Washington's favorite generals, Nathaniel Greene, was disowned for entering military service. Rufus Jones writes, "Even so blue-blooded a Friend as Nathaniel Greene of Rhode Island—a patriot of the patriots—had his name expunged from the list of members for the offence of "taking up arms" (Jones 2004, 151). Barbour writes, "Ex-Quakers ultimately proved good soldiers, providing the Americans with two colonels and three generals, of whom the most famous was Rhode Island's Nathaniel Greene" (Barbour 1988, 141).

Quakers treasure the teachings of Jesus and Paul: "But I say to you, Love your enemies and pray for those who persecute you, so that you may be sons of your Father who is in heaven; for he makes his sun rise on the evil and on the good, and sends rain on the just and on the unjust" (Matt. 5:44) and "But I say to you that hear, Love your enemies, do good to those who hate you, pray for those who abuse you". (Luke 6:27–28).

Paul wrote, "See that none of you repays evil with evil, but always seek to do good to one another and to all" (Thess. 5:15). Also "Beloved, never avenge yourselves, but leave it to the wrath of God; for it is written, 'Vengeance is mine, I will repay, says the Lord'" (Rom. 12:19).

Both of my parents grew up in Wilburite Quaker families. The Peace Testimony was a major element in their faith. My father made an important contribution as a non-combatant at Camp Sherman during the 1918 flu epidemic. Even though he was only in his twenties, he reorganized the camp hospital. I have a letter he had written in which he said he would have gotten stripes if he had not been a conscientious objector. He did not have to march in drills, but when I was hiking with him, he would get into a marching step, and I would join. It was one of the proudest accomplishments of his life. He treasured a photo of himself in his uniform.

When I was of draft age, I went to Mexico to build a school in a village in an American Friends Service Committee work camp. I was classified as 1-O for alternative service in the national health, safety, and interest. It was exciting to live in San Pedro Tlaltenango, within sight of Popocatepetl, in a totally unfamiliar environment. We sat on the ground and used hammers to break volcanic rock into gravel. This was to save money and use the methods chosen by the village.

Both my brothers did alternative service. One worked in a mental hospital, which was a bit of a worry for my mother.

When I was in grade school during World War II, a neighborhood boy dropped a wooden model of a tommy gun into our yard. It had a crank, which made the sound of machine gun fire. I picked it up, but Mother took it away and sent me to my room. We were never, ever allowed to play with guns. I was very angry and banged my fist into the beautiful mirror in my bedroom. Mother never mentioned the incident. And I learned a lesson about forgiveness.

Our family rarely went to movies, and when we did, we saw only those without violence. We never saw Disney's *Snow White and the Seven Dwarves* because the witch was too violent.

Young Quaker men often strayed from Quaker peace principles. Some of my Blackburn ancestors in Pennsylvania went off to fight Indians. They never encountered Indians but were disowned from membership. Once they repented, they were accepted back into membership.

A story is told about a Quaker in the Pennsylvania Assembly. As a joke, his fellow lawmakers elected him to head the State Militia. He became famous when he commanded, "Troops, ground your arms."

A story is told of a Quaker farmer who was having difficulties with a cow. He warned the cow, "Thee knows I will not beat thee, but if thee does not cooperate, I will sell thee to a Presbyterian who will beat thee."

When we were young, peace among the Blackburn children had a special meaning. My two older brothers knew how to torment me and my sister without touching us: they told us that we were ignorant. This was a serious affront for children of a college professor.

3

Promote Social Justice

My parents were active with social justice. Daddy served on the board of directors of the Godman Guild, a part of the Settlement House movement, which gave assistance to immigrants. Camp Mary Orton was operated by Godman Guild to serve the low-income community of Columbus, Ohio. We often got calls from people who wanted to seek Dr. Blackburn's advice. We would go hiking in the ravines near Camp Mary Orton.

Some Quaker conferences were held at the camp, thanks to Daddy's work on the boards of directors of a variety of welfare organizations. His position as professor of public administration (social welfare) at Ohio State University gave him many connections with these organizations.

Our parents welcomed refugees such as the Abolins from Latvia. When an interracial couple who were members of the Quaker meeting had difficulties with neighbors, our parents would go to their house to be a comforting presence.

Our parents were active on committees of the American Friends Service Committee (AFSC), the main social activist organization of American Quakers. The AFSC was set up after the First World War to give assistance in war-torn countries. Famine relief and clothing assistance were part of the work. The AFSC organized work camps all over the world, an important model for the Peace Corps. Even at Earlham College, we students would go on weekends to work in inner city neighborhoods, with organizations such as Flanner House in Indianapolis. I worked in an AFSC work camp in San Pedro Tlaltenango in Mexico constructing a school entirely with hand tools.

The Friends Committee on National Legislation (FCNL) was the lobbying arm of American Quakers and had a high profile with Congress, often giving extensive testimony on issues of peace and social justice.

Mother was active in various marches, including "leafleting" near movie theaters showing antiwar films like *On the Beach*, *Dr. Strangelove*, and *Seven Days in May*.

A friend reminded me that Mother went on a Poor People's March. There was a silent march in Washington sponsored by the AFSC. When I worked as administrative assistant to the executive secretary of the Dayton Regional Office of the AFSC, my boss reminded me not to chatter while walking in order not to disrupt the solemnity of the march, which gained national press attention.

A poignant memory is of when a member of the North Columbus Friends Meeting was dying of cancer. My parents and other members would spend hours sitting by her bedside.

My parents made financial contributions to many good causes. I get solicitations from the Southern Poverty Law Center.

4

Treasure Your Quaker and Family Connections

QUAKERS ARE NOT EXTREMELY clannish, but we keep in close touch with our relatives. This is partly because we are a very small religious minority, which in the seventeenth and eighteenth centuries suffered grievously for our faith. Whalen reports that "between 1650 and 1689 more than 450 Quakers died in prison for their religious beliefs, and at least 15,000 spent time in prison" (Whalen 1991, 18). They had a Meeting for Sufferings, which provided help to families with members in prison and kept a careful record of the price Quakers paid for their beliefs. A record in the minutes of the Meeting for Sufferings is the first known record of our ancestor, John Blackburn, who came to America in 1736 from Ireland. The Parliament in London had abolished tithes, but a local priest had so much power he ignored the law and took a horse from John in payment.

Mother and Daddy were founders of the North Columbus Friends Meeting and were active in many Quaker groups. In a letter, Daddy wrote,

> We had over 400 miles of beautiful country on our way to the Lake Erie Association (Quaker) conference in western Pennsylvania. The big camp where the meetings were held was very interesting, too, as it had many varieties of ferns, mosses and trees rarely found in Ohio. It is just at the edge of the Allegheny National Forest. There were springs, deep ravines, caves, a small lake for boating, etc. The children had fun hiking, playing at the lake and toasting marshmallows over an open fire. We had interesting accounts of each of the Meetings represented at the conference, and saw many friends who had come to the conference here at Columbus last year.

We children were birthright (automatic) members of both Ohio Yearly Meeting and Iowa Yearly Meeting, both being conservative Wilburite bodies. They were conservative in keeping the traditional silent worship of the Quakers in England but very liberal, even radical, on social causes such as race relations and peace. We Blackburns had four second cousins and a first cousin who attended Scattergood Friends School.

Mollie, Bill, and I went to Quaker colleges. Mollie and I attended Earlham College, and Bill attended Wilmington. Tom attended Bluffton College, a Mennonite school.

Daddy wrote, "He seems to be much interested in the difference between Mennonite religious beliefs and customs and those of Friends."

The North Columbus Friends Meeting held Monthly Meetings for Business at the homes of members. This meant extra house cleaning when our family was hosting. Mother wrote,

> I cleaned the bathroom, Mollie's and Walton's rooms last week after the Millsap children left on Tues. and now I must get the rest of the house gone over. I want to 'chem-tone' the stairway again as the little kids 'did

it much damage'! Monthly Meeting
will be here next Sunday.

These potluck dinners were special because
there was always a great variety of dishes brought by
each family in an effort to impress us all with their
wonderful cooking skills. I always had a very, very
good appetite.

Daddy wrote,

> I was put on the Olney Friends
> Boarding School Committee again
> for another three year term, and
> enjoyed the meetings. A number of
> people said they wished you would
> decide to come to Olney for your last
> two years. Anna Kirk especially said
> so. James Walton was sorry not to see
> you again this time.

Anna Kirk was our second cousin. I was named
after James Walton, a prominent member of Ohio
Yearly Meeting.

Mother wrote,

> Jim McDowell wanted to study
> for Ph.D. exam so Daddy took all

four children to Meeting," which he did not mind as he dearly loved little children. Jim and Nancy McDowell were active in the Meeting, and we kept in touch with them over the years. Jim eventually worked at Earlham, where he gave me a vocational aptitude test when I was wrestling with what I wanted to study. Nancy had worked at the Friends School in Ramallah, Jordan, many years earlier.

Auntie Florence once took Mollie, Tom, and me to spend Spring Vacation from Scattergood with Uncle Arthur Young, Mother's brother, in Rockford, Illinois. I have a photograph of my cousin Gary Young and me both on a bicycle with fishing rods. I was amazed at how many fish there were in the muddy little streams. Florence once took us bird watching and was extremely excited to see a Rose Breasted Grosbeak. Tom was not as avid a bird watcher as Bill, who kept detailed records of every bird he saw each year and a Life List of every species he had seen in his life. Tom had a great sense of humor and said he was very excited to see a "black-eyed warbler," a name he invented.

Quaker boarding schools were important to Blackburn children. Daddy wrote,

> I'm enclosing a copy of the Newsletter (North Columbus Meeting) as it has several items of special interest. We very much enjoyed the visit from Leanore and the four students (Alice Michener, Earl George, Loral Larson and Robert Hinshaw). Leanore reports that both of you are getting along well and things generally are prospering at school. I guess she was a little bit disappointed in their Olney Friends School visit, altho she thought they all learned some new things of interest. An exchange of students for several weeks would be better. Olney needs to have two real good representatives of Scattergood to attend there a year so to correct some misimpressions they have gotten. [Hint: He wants Mollie and me to go there our last two years.] Mollie, does thee write to or hear from Anna Kirk: it

would be interesting for both of you
to compare school notes.

Daddy wanted us to attend Olney, but because
Olney did not have music and Scattergood did,
Mother won the argument for Scattergood, where
she had attended, which I did not learn until I
read it in Berquist's book. I also learned there that
Mother's sister, Auntie Florence, had been a teacher
there.

Mother was an excellent photographer and
showed her love for all of us by with dozens of family pictures. She had a 620-film camera, which tele-
scoped out with bellows. One shot, probably staged,
was of a goat "pulling a wagon" with Mollie and me,
about age three, with Bill holding up an ear of corn
to tempt the goat to move. She once snapped a can-
did shot of me butting heads with a goat on a long
plank. I had leaned up against the goat house. To
my utter surprise, even though I had left the goat
back in the pasture, a half hour later, I found the
goat munching on the garden, which would have
horrified Daddy.

I get a kick at looking at family pictures because
Daddy always looks deadly serious—sometimes he
even had his hat on. It might date back to the time
when film was very slow and people had to hold a

very still pose for many seconds. This may account for people looking very tired and serious in old photographs. I never liked to grin for the camera because I felt that it was not authentic.

Once I visited a distant cousin in a Quaker retirement home. I made some comment and casually used the word *gee*. ("Gee whiz" was popular.) My cousin admonished me that this was akin to swearing because it was shorthand for *Jesus*.

We never had a TV until 1960 so that Daddy could watch the Kennedy-Nixon debate. I remember with great pleasure that Daddy would read great classic literature aloud to Mother. He was a very gifted storyteller and was very popular with the children at Quaker conferences. Mother did not like the extreme violence in these classic folk and fairytales.

Daddy kept in close contact with relatives. He wrote, "Bill, Tom, Phillip Miller and I had a very pleasant trip home, stopping at Uncle Henry Blackburn's, north of Indianapolis, near Westfield, Indiana, overnight, and we had a good hot breakfast."

I found out many years later, while visiting Leanna Barker Roberts, who had been on a Peace Caravan I helped to organize in the summer of 1963 (we heard Dr. King say his "I Have a Dream" speech in person), that my Great Uncle Henry had lived on the farmstead just across the road from them. I remembered that Daddy told me that he had spent years on that farm with his grandfather, Abel Hewitt Blackburn. His father, William J. Blackburn, Sr. who was a homeopathic physician in Salem, Ohio, thought that the climate was better for his health than the often overcast weather in Ohio.

Daddy wanted to study horticulture originally, but his sympathy for children led to social work. His first cousin, Ruth Blackburn Richardson, was a nurse whom Willa and I visited in 2006 for her one hundredth birthday at Hoosier Village north of Indianapolis. We have a photo showing us holding a birthday cake. She had been very close to Daddy as they were both much more educated than most others in the family.

Daddy reported the arrival of a new first cousin, Robert Pittfield Lovett V, a child of Robert, son of Daddy's sister, Caroline Blackburn Lovett. Daddy and I took a trip by Greyhound Bus to the east coast to visit Caroline in 1950; we visited Baltimore and DC, and I took photos of buildings from the top of the Washington Monument with my little Ansco 120 box camera. We visited cousins Robert and Helen Lovett on the banks of the Delaware River, and I have a photo of Daddy helping to dig out a basement for a house extension.

Robert was an expert cabinetmaker and must have done well as they had a large house on the Delaware River. Years later, in an exchange of annual letters, they told me about going to a Blackburn Family Association event, but so many descendants of the John Blackburn who came over from Ireland in 1736 were there that they had a difficult time finding any close relatives.

Bill Lovett lived in the Glen Gardner intentional community in New Jersey, which had a very left-ist press called The Libertarian Press. A first cousin once removed, Linn Lovett, attended Scattergood.

A special event for us children was our Sunday afternoon hikes with Daddy up to the C and O railroad tracks. We waved to the train crews of a passenger, a mixed freight, a long coal train bound for Toledo, and two 150-car empty trains returning to the coal fields in West Virginia and Kentucky. Daddy wrote, "As you will remember, the engineers, firemen and brakemen nearly always wave to the children as they go by, to the great delight of the youngsters. Can you remember how you felt ten years or so ago?"

We had a family joke about a conductor from a caboose wanting to take my sister home with him. Once when Daddy went on the Sportsman to Toledo on a consulting job, he waved a white hankie out the back platform for us to see. "I thought of you and how much I always enjoyed these hikes with all of you." In later years, I was very excited to be invited to get aboard a steam locomotive.

Our family was close-knit although I never had any appreciation for this when I was young and never dreamed any families were not like us. When Mollie and I were off at Scattergood Friends School in Iowa, Bill was at Wilmington College and Tom was at Bluffton College, we got letters once a week from Mother and Daddy, and they expected us to write home once a week. Mother would then type out each of our letters on onion skin paper with carbon copies and send each of us a copy. Mother's and Daddy's letters would entirely fill the pages. I treasure ten letters from 1950. In a letter dated October 16, 1950, Mother wrote, "You will be justified in sending us a telegram to see if we are sick if we don't get this letter off soon." She advised Mollie and me that if one is feeling ill and does not feel like writing, "Do ask the other to write."

Once, our parents wrote, "Well, perhaps this letter will be long enough to make up for being so late. Both of your recent letters were exceptionally interesting and enjoyable. We count a lot on getting them the middle of each week. We could enjoy a word from thee too Bill. Mother made chocolate cake with icing and candles for my birthday. Much love, Dad and Mother (with both signatures).

In another letter, "We hope to hear form <u>All of You</u> again soon, and to see you, Bill and Tom on or before thanksgiving. How we do wish the twins could be here, too. Mollie, do write to Cousin Anna, and see if thee can't keep in touch with Olney affairs that way. I should go to the next meeting of the Olney big committee, in Twelfth Month, if I can make it. Much love to all, Mother and Daddy." Daddy was on the Olney School Committee for years.

"11-23-50 - Home - 4:30 pm Dears, I wanted to get a letter there on Scattergood Day, but I don't know whether this will get off today or not."

*****

Many Visits from Dear Family Members

Bill came with Fred and Dor last eve at 7 o'clock, and after we ate bean soup, kale and spice chiffon cake Fred, Bill and Daddy went to meet Tom, who arrived at 8:30 pm. We visited till after 10 and went to bed. It surely was good to see Tom. He seems to be feeling alright. Rest of us are chipper. Mr.

Pantacol was our company. He and Daddy have gone for a walk, Fred is working on his car, Bill is reading, Tom doing [weather] maps [he became a professional meteorologist], Dor reading and eating pecans and all are listening to the Missouri and Kansas game. We had roast rooster, mashed potatoes, collards, cranberries, Jello salad of cranberries, apples and oranges ground up and plum pudding. Ray is outdoors playing. I am to go babysit tonight at 8 o'clock. It is the first place I went and the boy was asleep when I got there so I had nothing to do for him. On Sat I am to go at 12:30 pm and stay till they get back from an evening party, so I expect it will be about 12 hours. I went Mon night again to the Casparros where are 2 babies at 6:30 and staid till 12:30. Then I am to go on next Wed at 9 am to care for a 15 mths old girl while her mother goes downtown.

*****

When does Christmas vacation begin? We will look up bus schedules for you. It would take longer than the train but you probably would not have to change stations in Chicago. [I remember in a bus station in Davenport hearing the night hawks clicking sounds and thinking of how Alice Michener would enjoy it.] Let us know just what time of day and what day you are free and we will look up the best route and send the money. Walton, does thee know that Orie Edgerton is a distant cousin? Their home sounds very interesting. We are glad thee went to visit with Cousin Jessie [Blackburn] Jones." [She operated a variety store in West Branch, Iowa and was famous because she addressed all customers with the plain language of the Quakers]. I learned to type at a Business College in Cedar Rapids, but I did not quite finish so I am not very speedy or efficient. This was soon after I finished High School. [According to the Scattergood history book, Mother was at Scattergood at one time, maybe not to graduate—and her sister, Florence was a teacher. Mother also went to Westtown, an elite Quaker boarding school near Philadelphia where a cousin of hers, Daniel Test, was Headmaster—she was a bit scornful of him as I think he looked down upon her as a bit of a "rustic" with her Iowa country Quaker manners.] Now Mr. Pantacol is ready to go so I will send this hoping Daddy can find a place where it will be picked up tonight. Love, Mother.

Once when we visited our second cousin, Anna, on her father's farm in eastern Ohio, she played a trick on Tom because he was so bossy. One of our tasks was to pick off the webs of worms, which were harming bushes. She made up to punish Tom for his bossiness a requirement that he had to squash each of the worms.

Yearly trips from Ohio to Whittier, Iowa, were a great treat. Our grandmother Mary Mott Young, Auntie Florence, and Cousins Dorothy and Charlotte would spoil us children with great affection and funny stories. For example, "Rudolph, the Red (Communist), knows rain (weather observation), dear."

Mother loved having her sister, Florence, living in Wilmington, Ohio. She wrote, "We were really thrilled to have Aunt Florence, Bill, Anna Lee, and Fred and Dorothy come Sunday evening." Visiting from near Eugene, Oregon, were Gerald and Eva Mae Bowerly, who was Mother's cousin, who "showed us slides of their family of five children and seven grandchildren."

Daddy wrote, "Walton, he is quite a farmer and mill man, who was something of a pioneer out there. We looked at thy popcorn and thought that quite a little of it may ripen ok. It is still standing as I hope it will continue to harden up. When it is cut and shocked the rats get into it."

Mother boarded children to raise money for our tuition at Scattergood Friends School. Daddy, who loved all children, wrote, "I hear the baby crying, so must go up and look after her. Much love, Daddy." He had been neglected by his own mother, which gave him great sympathy for children. When I traveled with him, if he heard a baby crying, he would often offer to hold the baby and comfort him or her, for which many mothers were grateful. These were the days before one had to worry about some stranger kidnapping a child.

5

Show Your Faith in Daily Life

SERVICE TO OTHERS IS one of the best ways to worship God and help bring the kingdom of heaven on earth.

For the Blackburn family, talking about our faith was not as important as acting out our Quaker heritage each day.

Faith is not to be proclaimed from the rooftops but is shown day by day. We show our faith by who we are. Actions speak louder than words. Even in how we treat our fellow creatures and our animals. Latitia was my very affectionate pet chicken who ran to me instantly when I got home from school. She loved to be carried around in my arms. Our milk goats were part of the family. They thought they were people, and each had a distinctive personality.

Just as important as grand schemes to improve the world are the little daily connections we make with our fellow human beings. Our faith in practice makes the world a better place.

Jesus said, "In the world you have tribulation; but be of good cheer, I have overcome the world" (John: 16-33).

My father's favorite Bible passage was "He has showed you O man, what is good; and what does the LORD require of you but to do justice, and to love kindness, and to walk humbly with your God?" (Micah: 6:8).

My grandmother Mary Mott Young would have scripture reading and meditation every morning after breakfast.

Catholic mysticism was compatible with Quaker mysticism. I once carried around in my pocket *A Guide to True Peace or the Excellency of Inward and Spiritual Prayer*, compiled chiefly from the writings of the Catholic mystics, Fenelon, Guyon, and Molinos: "This little book was written to nourish the spiritual life. Evidently it succeeded in its purpose, for it passed through at least twelve editions and re-printings from 1813 to 1877. Compiled anonymously by two Quakers, William Backhouse and James Janson, from the writings of three great mystics of a century earlier, Fenelon, Guyon, and Molinos, it was widely used as a devotional book by members of the Society of Friends" (vii).

I treasure a favorite saying of Dr. Martin Luther King: "The long arc of the moral universe bends toward justice." I heard in person his speech "I Have a Dream" at the Lincoln Memorial. I had helped to organize a Young Friends Peace Caravan which visited Quaker meetings and churches in the Midwest.

We Blackburns treasure the Great Commandment: "You shall love the Lord your God with all your heart, and with all your soul, and with all you mind. This is the great and first commandment. And a second is like it, You shall love our neighbor as yourself. On these two commandments depend all the law and the prophets" (Matt. 22:36-40).

6

Practice Quaker Simplicity, Frugality, and Self-Sufficiency with a Healthy Country Lifestyle

In the country, we had lots of sunshine, fresh air, space to run, and fresh vegetables and fruits. We helped Daddy in our large gardens. Mother once complained, however, that Daddy was too particular about our help when we were little and restricted our help.

We had large maple trees for climbing and swings, a slide, and a sandbox. Animals were a dog, a donkey, cats, goats, and my pet chicken, Latitia.

We had an area we called Playtown; it was an area of yellow clay where the topsoil had been stripped off to build the causeway of the North Broadway bridge approach. Bill was the chief engineer, which later on became his profession. We made roads by rubbing down paths to look like asphalt and had sticks along the edges as guard rails.

We greatly treasured Sunday nature walks when Daddy taught us the names of the wildflowers. We got very excited about the beautiful stones in the gravel road but were disappointed to learn—just Rose Quartz.

We built dams in a creek. We caught crayfish but had to watch out for their huge claws. The water striders or water spiders scurried and skipped across the surface to avoid getting eaten by minnows.

There were pastures with blackberry bushes. One summer, my neighbor and I took gallon paint cans and very innocently filled them with blackberries, never thinking about getting permission. We went by Ms. Power's house and showed them to her. She was very distraught that we had picked the bushes she had been saving for friends. We slunk home too, ashamed to tell Mother, but Ms. Power telephoned Mother to apologize for scolding us. Murder will out!

I roamed around at night. Two neighbor boys and I went to a pasture and looked at an upper window to see their cousin Barbara undressing for bed. She never appeared, but sneaking around in the dark was fun.

Mother used double boilers and pressure cookers on the coal stove to conserve heat. To start the stove, Daddy used a corn cob soaked in kerosene. In winter, Daddy would shake the furnace grates in the early morning to bring the coals to life and start heating the house. It filled the whole house with a terrible racket. Daddy shoveled coal from a huge pile in the driveway into the basement. A great treat was popping corn in a wire basket popper over the open fireplace.

Daddy was a great gardener, and we had all the Swiss chard, collards, and beet greens we could eat. He grew sweet and Irish potatoes. We always waited eagerly for sweet corn season. Breakfast started with oatmeal and finished with bacon and eggs from our own hens.

We got started with chickens when in first-grade class, we had an incubator with an egg for each student. Once they hatched, our family ended up with all the little chicks because we were the only family with a place for chickens. **My pet chicken, *Letitia*, was very affectionate and loved to be carried around.**

It was fun to go to the henhouse and feel under each hen for a warm egg. The hens were too timid to peck. When we had an abundance of chickens, we would sell them to people who wanted fresh country chicken. I would find it awesome when Daddy chopped off the heads and the headless bodies would flop around wildly.

We cornered an opossum in a manure pile. We discovered they are very brave with huge teeth.

We played endless hours of badminton and croquet. We had no TV. We were only allowed to listen to "The Shadow" and "Blondie" on the radio on Sunday night—never "The Lone Ranger." Mrs. Buff Orpington told Dagwood that her husband was "The man who invented the chicken, you know." Buff Orpington is a popular chicken breed.

My parents had married in the Great Depression and were very frugal. When our parents killed and canned a male goat kid and one which was a hermaphrodite (our brothers pronounced it "morphadite"), my sister and I refused to eat our former playmates. When the goats were not producing much milk, Mother and Daddy would sit for hours shaking large class jars to liquefy powdered milk. We mixed yellow packets to make margarine look like butter.

My parents never had a TV set until the election of 1960 when Daddy wanted to watch the Kennedy-Nixon debate.

Gardening was Daddy's hobby. We got fresh vegetables from two huge gardens. It was his stress relief from teaching. Daddy loved to experiment—he had cotton and was fascinated just to watch the bolls develop. We had cabbage, broccoli, asparagus, Swiss chard, mustard, collards, spinach, lettuce, beet greens, and parsley. These are very rich in vitamins. We also had lima, kidney, soy, and snap beans. He grew root crops like carrots, parsnips, beets, ruta-bagas, Irish, and sweet potatoes. Upland rice was without success. We had sweet corn, varieties of tomatoes, watermelons, cantaloupes, yellow summer squash, and acorn squash.

Mother's famous soy bean bread, sweetened with our own Sorghum Molasses, were a rich source of protein. We ground up the dry beans with an antique hand-cranked coffee grinder. Mother was ahead of her time in her knowledge of nutrition. Daddy also grew salsify, onions, and okra. When I interviewed for a job in Tennessee, the interviewer was very impressed when I ordered a dish with okra. He was surprised that I even knew about their southern food.

Daddy delighted the secretaries at Ohio State with bouquets of gladiolas, dahlias, iris, daffodils, narcissus, and jonquils. We'd know that spring had arrived when we saw the yellow forsythia. Orange poppies and peonies lined the driveway. Purple, yellow, and white crocuses meant winter was over.

We never ever, ever had soft drinks—with one exception. A great treat was going to a dairy store in the country to get ice cream, and we'd put ginger ale on it. We made our own ice cream with an old-fashioned crank. In winter, Mother made snow cream.

Daddy grew sorghum cane. We'd stripped off the leaves one night. The next morning, we'd cut the stalks and trucked them to a farmer with a roller mill powered by a circling horse. The cane juice was boiled into molasses. Mother's famous soybean bread with molasses was way ahead of its time for good nutrition.

Our parents believed in Quaker simplicity. When other students in University School received fancy gifts for Christmas, our family had modest, often home-made gifts.

The 1928 Model A Ford was our farm car, which we used to haul the goats. It had a hand crank for winter, which could give a good kick.

Mother canned hundreds of jars of tomatoes, corn, and snap beans. We spent hours cutting fresh corn off the cobs and snapping beans. We also had wild greens, such as lambs quarters, watercress, and dandelion—which were usually seen as weeds.

We bought ice, which we'd place in our ice box. When the land we rented was sold for the Riverside Hospital, our parents moved into Columbus and had the luxury of an electric refrigerator and clothes dryer.

We did not conform to the values of the early Quakers as we had a Christmas tree with colored lights, icicles, ornaments, popcorn strings, and brightly wrapped packages. We never, ever believed in Santa Clause; that is in violation of Quaker truthfulness. We also rejected rampant materialism.

Simplicity went out the window at Thanksgiving. We had turkey and all the trimmings. Minced-meat pie was topped with home-made ice cream. We had elderberry jam from wild bushes.

I was pleased to find in a letter to us at Scattergood that Mother and Daddy had gone to see Steamboat Round the Bend with Will Rogers. Mother never let us see *Snow White and the Seven Dwarves* because of violence. We could go to see *My Friend Flicka* and *Lassie Come Home*. I sneaked away to see *She Wore a Yellow Ribbon* with neighbors.

We always turned off lights when we left a room. Even today, the Queen of England turns off lights in the Royal Palace.

We were fond of recycling. Daddy assembled discarded wagon parts into an odd-looking, but usable children's wagons. I was horribly embarrassed when Daddy and I went to a local dump for toy parts. A man said, "Look, Pops, you are not allowed to be here. So get out."

When we traveled, we camped at state parks or stayed in tourist homes. Mother would put peanut butter on cabbage for snacks on the road.

7

Treasure Education

EDUCATION GIVES SKILLS TO make the world a better place.

Quakers were pioneers in education in America. Two universities founded by Quakers were Cornell and Johns Hopkins. Prestigious Quaker colleges include Earlham, Wilmington, Swarthmore, Haverford, William Penn, Guilford, Bryn Mawr, George Fox, Whittier, Malone, Friends University, Azusa Pacific University, and Barclay.

Education was very important to the early Quakers because they wanted their children to get a guarded education, away from the pernicious materialism of mainstream culture. They established schools when they built meetinghouses on the American frontier. The schools met in the meetinghouses until a school building could be built. Quaker concern for education created an environment for several prominent Quaker scientists, inventors, and industrialists in England. Quakers were denied entry into Cambridge and Oxford for refusal to swear oaths. They went to Scotland where John Knox wanted all Presbyterians to be able to read the Bible, creating the Scottish Renaissance.

Education was always very important in our family. Mother had training in kindergarten education and was featured in a Boston newspaper as director of a child care center.

I remember hearing Daddy read great literature to Mother after we went to bed. One of our favorite card games was Authors.

Daddy was professor of social work at Ohio State. When we were children, we had savings bank accounts for college. Our parents, in accord with gentle Quaker principles, never pressured us to excel. Until we went to college, we had never had letter grades, but only written reports. Mother said she never told us our IQ scores so we would not be jealous.

I had nerd tendencies in grade school. One summer, I read a biology book written by a friend of Daddy. At Scattergood, I spent several Saturdays in the library reading Russian history. We considered comics to be mind-polluting trash. I was quite astonished to find a dear schoolmate at Scattergood following Li'l Abner in each Sunday paper.

The following article appeared in *The Olney Current* dated 04-1937. Daddy was on the Olney Friends School Committee and wanted us to attend there rather than Scattergood. Mother prevailed, however, because Olney had no music.

A Religiously Guarded Education, by William Blackburn, Jr.

Our Boarding School was established to insure a religiously guarded education beyond the primary years, for Friends' children. Is it needed today? When one looks at the rampant war spirit, the drift toward nationalism and materialism, the decay of personal standards of morality and honesty which have accompanied the almost complete secularization of public education, and considers what part of the lack of religious or moral training may have played in the process, can he doubt the answer to that question? Never before was there greater need to conserve and pass on to our children the splendid religious and moral heritage that characterizes all consistent Friends. The Boarding School plays a large and important part in this. Perhaps to fulfill this function properly there might be a course covering specifically the history of our Society, considering the reasons for its founding, the outstanding principles which have characterized our Quaker message and their application to the problems of today. Let this be no formal course in church history, but a dynamic approach to the study of current history, taught by one having a deep spiritual experience of the application of Quaker principles in his own daily life, a sympathetic understanding of the aspiration of youth, and a broad knowledge of the underlying causes of our present social and economic maladjustments. I would hope that each student derived from the course something of the courage and ability to give a good account of the faith that was in him which imbued the founders of our Society. The world needs such to lead it out of the slough of despond. Our children will need this courage to face troubled years ahead.

Experience with hundreds of students from every size and kind of public high school convinces me that a relatively small boarding school has very marked advantages over the usual day high school. Every normal young person must sometime break the sheltering home ties and go out to face the world alone. Our boarding school offers unexcelled opportunity to make this break with a minimum of strain on the slowly maturing social and religious character of youth. Association with other students from homes animated with ideals similar to his own and close personal contact, in the classroom and in the many affairs of daily life, with a faculty deeply interested in his religious and social development as well as in his intellectually advancement, give him the best possible chance to make the readjustment from home to the outside world successfully. Nor would I discount the great value of high standards of teaching possible in such a school. Small classes, where teacher and students may exchange ideas and discuss all angles of the topics assigned for study, promote a thoroughness of understanding not possible in large, formal and perpetually rushed schedules of most high schools. Every student needs to be stimulated to think his way through each problem from beginning to end, never content to accept half-understood facts or principles simply because some author or textbook or some teacher has stated them to be so.

Whether a student plans to go to college or to return to a chosen occupation after graduating, his success depends on the quality rather than the quantity of his education. A few good tools well-handled are the crying need of today. Let him take along relatively few facts, but those thoroughly well understood; a small number of underlying principles and natural laws, with their application to life appreciated: an ability to read understandingly, to write legibly and concisely, to perform the four basic operations of arithmetic quickly and certainly; an appreciation of the beauties of nature and of human, character and goodness; a fundamental intellectual honesty in facing every issue; with this equipment he need have no fear in going forth to whatever life he has chosen.

I am convinced that our Friends" Boarding School can and should be able to give its graduates the foregoing advantages to a degree rarely possible elsewhere. Were half the students who attend our classes at the University thus well-equipped a large percentage of the academic and moral failures here might be avoided. I hope that my own four children may be privileged to attend Olney in due course, and I crave for them the wholesome daily life, the splendid inspiration of fine teachers and supervisors, the sound educational advantages and the happy memories that I treasure as a precious heritage of my own days at Boarding School.

8

Love All Nature and Animals

OUR PARENTS KNEW HOW to care for farm animals. They had a tender regard for all animals as God's creatures. Daddy spoke of the little creatures and was very gentle with any young or injured wild animal. He grew up with horses and once plowed the garden with a horse. I thought nothing of it at the time, but years later, I asked my brother about it, and he said that it was because the horse did not pack the soil as much as the tractors. Daddy usually paid our truck garden neighbors to plow the gardens.

Mother wrote in a letter of a kitten crawling on her neck. "The kitten is trying to type and actually stepped on the spacer and moved it twice. It has fleas and I'm trying to get rid of them. Now the cat is on my shoulder, peacefully observing the typing. Hope I don't get fleas."

Bill and Tom milked the goats twice a day. Bill painted a beautiful goat sign, which hung along Olentangy River Road. People who could not digest cow's milk wanted naturally homogenized goat milk. Mother pasteurized and cooled the milk quickly to avoid any goat flavor.

Raising goats was a way of life. We loved each with her very distinctive personality; they were very affectionate and thought they were people. When a goat needed to be bred, we loaded her into the back seat of the Model A Ford and took her to a farm with a buck. We observed "the facts of life."

People who raised goats all knew each other, and there was a *Dairy Goat Journal*. Mother grew up on a farm near Whittier, Iowa, and knew animal care. When we went to Iowa to visit Grandmother, we boarded the goats on a farm with other goats and knew that they would get excellent care. When the goat kids were able to walk, they were weaned from the mother. It was a challenge but great fun to teach them to drink from a pan. At first, they would get too much milk and snort and cough in a very delicate way until they learned to sip gently. Mother made a photo of a grimacing Tom holding a pan with three goat kids, each pushed the pan around hard in a different direction.

When the goat kids were able to run, Mother took them in to University School. The kindergarten children made a circle, and the goat kids danced around, nibbled on the shoelaces, and urinated on the floor to the delight of the children—but not the janitor.

Mother taught us birds who came to the feeder for Sunflower seeds. It was a thrill to see Baltimore orioles and goldfinches. Each spring, we marveled at the great V formations of the high flying Canada geese going north to nest and watched for their return to the Gulf Coast in the fall. How they talked to each other always fascinated us.

I treasure photos Mother took of us all stark naked wading in a creek. Daddy knew a huge cave in southern Ohio where we camped.

Daddy taught us weather lore. One of which is "Red sky at night, sailors' delight. Red sky in the morning, sailors take warning." We loved glorious sunrises, sunsets, and lightning. A special memory was lying on our backs for a huge meteor shower. We also learned the constellations.

We loved the double rainbows after a storm. We learned that ice crystals made the sun dogs on each side of the sun.

9

Have a Strong Work Ethic

WORK IS A MEANS to improve the world. "Work is love made visible," they say.

We always had summer jobs for college money. Mother and Daddy would take us to homes over in Columbus where we would mow lawns with push mowers. We worked in a tree nursery and truck gardens. I worked for Mr. Riggs, a schoolteacher who wanted the outdoor work for his health. He opened The Vitamin Shop. I slept on our front porch, and he would come at five in the morning, and we would go to the wholesale market downtown in Columbus to buy produce we did not grow. We planted hundreds of tomato plants and irrigated them with river water.

We put our earnings in a Savings Bank account for college. One summer, when I clerked at The Vitamin Shop, I drank lots of coke. We never, ever,

ever had carbonated drinks at home but cokes were just five cents. I spent way too much on the forbidden drink, and Mother never knew.

Mother was diligent and indulgent. She did laundry for Bill off at Wilmington College. She did a lot of sewing and was expert in knitting. I kept the beautiful sweaters she knit for me for many years. When she was at Sandy Spring Friends House nursing home and could barely speak any more, she told me just out of the blue in a strong voice that every stitch was done with love.

We had a cousin, Jessie Blackburn Jones, who operated a variety store in West Branch, Iowa. She was widely renown for using the plain language with all customers (Berquist 1990, 33). I exchanged annual letters with her granddaughter who told me that Grandmother would come home after a long day in the store and immediately work on sewing projects for the AFSC for needy folks. A remarkable work ethic, though typical of Iowa Quakers.

It has been said that "the Quakers came to America to do good and did well." They worked hard and were very frugal—a perfect formula for success in America. Their honesty rejected oath taking. Jesus said, "Let your yea be yea, and your nay be nay," and forbade all swearing as evil, as in

Matthew 5:33–37. Honesty in business meant asking and giving only what each article was worth.

Consistent pricing made Quakers respected, and "once persecutions were over it often made them rich" (Barbour). Quakers used "a one-price system in merchandising, which reflected their commitment to integrity both in the pricing and in the quality of goods and services offered for sale" (Cooper 2000, 166). Quakers "invented the price tag."

The deep commitment of English Friends to honesty led to stunning achievements in industry, management, and science. The idea that those barred from political power and subjected to serious discrimination will channel their creative efforts elsewhere was borne out of the eighteenth-century Quakers. Their reputation for honesty and fairness reassured outsiders that Friends were trustworthy. Plain living, dependable work habits, and inventiveness made them prosperous. Intermarriage among Quaker families meant that the capital accumulated by one generation was passed on. By the mid-eighteenth century English Quakers had become almost a clan of extended kinfolk bound together by patterns of commerce and religion (Barbour 1988, 86).

Many English Quakers became prominent merchants and bankers; they grew wealthy because of the trust they gained through honesty. They were known to scholars of management for paying "a living wage" and for looking out for the welfare of employees.

Quaker dynasties emerged in commerce. The Pease and Backhouse families and five generations of the Gurney family made fortunes in the woolen trade and manufacturing. The Barclays and Hanburys accumulated fortunes through trade with colonial America. Quakers became involved in the entire spectrum of English artisan, manufacturing, and commercial activities including pharmaceutical supplies, tinplating, smelting of lead, mining of copper and lead, and the brewing of beer (Barbour 1988, 87).

The eighteenth century saw the rise of Quaker banks: Freame and Barclay, Hoare's, Backhouse's, Gurney's, Lloyds, Pim's. Even after two centuries of mergers, two of the largest English banks, Barclays and Lloyds, retain the names of their Quaker founders (Barbour 1988, 87).

Quaker contributions in medicine include John Fothergill's clinical observations, helping inoculate people for smallpox with live vaccine, and helping found the London Medical Society. Fothergill promoted plans for humanitarian relief and civic improvements and corresponded with Friends in America about prison reform. Other Quakers showed that the use of cowpox was a safe way to inoculate against smallpox (Barbour, 87–88).

On a visit to Bluffton College, Daddy wrote, "Everyone we asked knew Tom and all spoke very highly of him as being a very good student and a fine chap in every way [Daddy's own inimitable dialect]. He was very modest about it, but I think he is enjoying college life very much. He does work too hard, but says the many outdoor jobs won't last much longer, so he must make hay while the sun shines. He sent home quite a lot of money to his account beside what he kept for his many day to day expenses."

Tom was one of the outstanding salespersons for Watkins Products—he was not afraid to go into the poorer Black neighborhoods. He was very friendly, extremely courteous, and respectful. I was not nearly as successful as Tom as I enjoyed listening to the tales of woe of the lonely housewives. But I did learn that being a door-to-door salesman was very, very hard work.

Section 4

Scattergood Friends School

IN MIDDLE AMERICA, THERE is an oasis of peace and love out in the middle of Iowa, a place where the religious values of the Quakers who came over with William Penn are vibrant. Scattergood Friends School near West Branch is up on a wind-swept hill. It is a community of great diversity and strong traditions of the Society of Friends. It is a shining example of how people of faith can live and work in harmony and show deep respect for each individual. The Quaker concept of the Inner Light within every person commands respect for all fellow human beings, no matter their status in life. The experience of this community shaped my life in ways I would not realize until I saw the outside world.

This was a very conservative environment. We had daily devotions after breakfast with readings from such classics as *On the Imitation of Christ* by Thomas à Kempis. This was deep mysticism for teenagers, but we accepted it without question as in harmony with our Quaker heritage. In Collection, we had presentations on great Christian leaders.

We had no personal radios on campus. The only radio on campus was the radio phonograph in the Social Room in the Main Building. The only recorded music played on campus was classical phonograph records, which could be played in the two hours before supper. Brahms's Hungarian Dances, the Bach Brandenburg concertos, and Enescu's Romanian Rhapsodies echoed through the halls of the Main Building.

In Evening Collection, a talk on the Life of Beethoven, with a symphony, gave us a deep hunger for classical music. On Easter and at Christmas, we gathered to listen reverently to Handel's Messiah. The only radio program shared in Evening Collection was the national election returns in 1952. Those of voting age went in to West Branch. Others helped with the elections as part of American and World Government classes. Eight members of the Berquist Junior-Senior Government class went to Tipton to hear Governor Beardsley and Representative

Thomas Martin give campaign speeches. Although Iowa Wilburite Quakers worshipped in the ancient tradition of Silent Meditation, they were very liberal on social and political issues—an expression of the Social Gospel related to Jesus's Sermon on the Mount.

My grandmother, Mary Mott Young, began each day with the reading of Scripture and silent meditation. The *thee* and *thou* of the King James Version of the Bible were used by Wilbuite Quakers in the traditional Quaker plain language used by all my Blackburn and Young relatives. Mary Mott Young was a distant relative of the husband of the famous suffragette Lucretia Mott. A Mott cousin sent me photographs of my grandmother Young in the Whittier, Iowa Meetinghouse in her antique traditional Quaker Bonnet. My Blackburn ancestor, John Blackburn, came from Armagh, Ireland, to Quaker Pennsylvania in 1736.

In an Interest Group, which met twice a week, we learned classics like "Sumer Is a Cumin In" and "English Country Gardens" from Nancy Taylor, a teacher with a gift for teaching music. This Interest Group made special presentations on Scattergood Day and at Commencement. Two of the very musically gifted boys sang "Cool Water" and "The Lord's Prayer" in the Boys' Dormitory over and over endlessly—the verses come easily to memory. Don sang "Ole Man River" in a deep bass voice on camping trips. He introduced me to the glorious Beethoven "Emperor" Piano Concerto. We all sang folk songs late into the night on our unforgettable and joyous fall and spring camping trips. A harmonica and a ukulele made special memories. Faculty members read spooky stories from Edgar Allen Poe. Some students were gifted tellers of folk and fairy tales.

We had absolutely no couple dancing. Saturday night folk and square dancing, however, led by Lois, was immensely enjoyed. Bashful teens could hold hands without danger of rejection.

I was at Scattergood in the 1950s. Much of this narrative is from *The Scattergood*, a mimeographed periodical sent to parents and alumni every four to six weeks. Subscribers were from all over the United States, including Quaker institutions. The mailing list was over two hundred.

This account was assembled by James Walton Blackburn. Comments add a personal perspective. It includes class poems and stories – Breaking rules - Leaving campus without permission. Sneaking out of the dorm just for the sake of getting away with it.

We did not know we were in "college prep."

All four Blackburns went off to Scattergood Friends School in Iowa at age fourteen. Only later did I realize what an extraordinary and life-changing experience this was. Also, what an exceptional and unusual school.

We learned our Quaker heritage through the History of Quakerism class and in daily Collection and exceptional guest speakers. Even though Iowa is far from the east where the majority of Quakers live, major figures and scholars of Quakerism made the long trip. Scattergood was known worldwide. Barbour writes about Scattergood "whose community spirit, shared work, and teaching have drawn many students from other branches of Quakerism" (Barbour 1988, 233).

Graduates of Quaker boarding schools are accepted at the most prestigious colleges in America, including Harvard and Radcliffe, and institutions described by Oliver as "Quaker-born colleges, twelve of which are members of the Friends Association of Higher Education, and two universities founded by Friends as non-sectarian institutions." (Cornell and Johns Hopkins)

1

Leanore Goodenow

LEANORE GOODENOW WAS A determining factor in what Scattergood became when it was reborn in 1945. Her outstanding qualities of leadership and Quaker character made her extremely effective at raising funds and obtaining gifts for the school. She had a unique story to tell about a community in which the majority of the work was done by students and where life was guided by ideals of harmony, simplicity, community, equality, and peace.

Down to Earth

Leanore was a wonder. Even though she was responsible for fundraising, reporting to the School Committee, giving presentations about Scattergood throughout the United States, recruiting students and faculty, and decisions on school discipline, she left early one morning for Whittier to pick pears that the sophomores had been unable to get the day before, then went camping with the juniors. What a sport! She also taught English, religion, and Bible classes. Just amazing, just amazing. Talk about work ethic. Ten bushels of pears from Whittier.

Sophomores had a special treat of a waffle breakfast in Leanore's office. Too much baking powder in the batter, but waffles eaten with gusto.

Twenty-Four-Hour Duty

Enormous credit and gratitude are due to the dedicated staff who worked at modest salaries with little personal privacy, with twenty-four-hour duty. They believed in the school's Quaker ideals, which Leanore articulated. We received an outstanding education—graduates went to elite colleges, including Harvard, Haverford, and Radcliffe as well as Quaker colleges such as Earlham, Friends University, Penn College, Whittier, Wilmington, and Guilford.

Craft Schools

In the summer of 1950, Leanore made an extensive trip through the South and to the West

Coast. She visited eight craft schools for guidance on how to develop crafts at Scattergood. These were Abingdon, Penland School of Handicrafts, Pi Beta Phi Settlement School, the Craft Center, Campbell Folk School, Allanstand, Black Mountain College, and Tuskegee Institute. She also visited two experimental communities with Friends in each—Celo and Macedonia.

She traveled from New Orleans to California to visit alumni, new students, and parents of students to make contacts for prospective teachers and students and to renew friendships. She had a rich exchange of ideas and warm fellowship at Quaker centers and schools, including Pacific Ackworth, Pacific Oaks, the Verde Valley School in Arizona, the Peninsula School near San Francisco, and the Tracy Community. She attended First Day Meeting at Pasadena and visited with former staff of the Scattergood Hostel. She was in Fairhope, Alabama, for First Day Meeting and went to two picnics with Friends' groups. The primary school was of special interest.

Iowa Quakers and Scattergood

Delegations of students and Leanore, or a faculty member, attend many Iowa Quarterly meetings and talk about Quakerism in action at Scattergood.

Many Jobs on Trip

Leanore left Scattergood in May 1953, but not for vacation. She visited Earlham College and spoke with Raymond Wilson, next commencement speaker. She visited Mary Hoxie Jones and former teachers, graduates, and parents. She ordered new Maladur tableware and brought Enrique Gutierrez to visit. His father is a permanent member of the United Nations. We listened with wonder at all she did in two weeks.

Am I Mature, Cultured, Courteous, Enthusiastic?

"The time has come," the Walrus said, "to speak of many things." Meaning "college, college, college" and application blanks. For faculty, this means letters that read, "So and so has made application for entrance into our halls of higher learning, and we have been referred to you for information regarding his character and scholastic ability." These people want to know all about us and list certain characteristics for the faculty member to underline. One Sunday evening, Leanore told us of some of the asked-about characteristics. Am I cultured, mature, courteous, undisciplined, or enthusiastic? Am I generous? Do I tend to be deceitful? We must examine ourselves carefully.

Quaker Values with Edward Bear

Wilburite Quaker youth do not get formal indoctrination. We learned Quaker values from overhearing our parents talk with other Quakers and non-Quakers. At Scattergood, we learned Quaker values in courses on Quakerism, the Bible, and especially the New Testament. We studied the Apostle Paul and the Prophets. Every day, the entire school of roughly forty students assembled for Collection.

Among favorite experiences there was the director, Leanore Goodenow, reading the Little Stories of Saint Francis of Assisi (Housman) and the gentle wisdom of Winnie the Pooh. In history and social studies classes, we had weekly presentations by students of articles on current events. Without formal indoctrination, we had an intense dose of Quaker values. Scattergood was accused by the local veteran's organization of playing footsie with the Reds, when Jerome Davis spoke on Russia. This did not bother Scattergood's director, Leanore, in the slightest and gained sympathy for the school through the media.

2

Classes Are Fun—Wordsworth to Welding to Byzanetine Culture

Flexible Academic Program Due to Leanore

LEANORE LOBBIED IOWA EDUCATIONAL authorities to use teachers without standard credentials and to have a curriculum without some courses, such as chemistry. Her arguments were based upon graduates' acceptance and performance at demanding colleges and grades on qualifying tests.

Leanore was charismatic and deeply spiritual. She had the backing of Iowa Yearly Meeting (Conservative). Iowa Quakers are esteemed for integrity.

The academic program was very flexible. The teachers were very innovative and creative. They were dedicated to Quaker values. Academic standards were high—each student performed to his or her potential.

I got a comment, "There is no point in handing in such slipshod work as you will simply have to do it over again."

We did not receive letter grades, but we always received comments like, "Walton could do better if he applied himself more."

Also "Walton has improved in keeping his room more tidy, but there is still room for improvement."

Because of the small student body, students of different grades were mixed. Spanish class had sophomores, juniors, and seniors. Students in biology did independent study at a college level. I studied ferns and hydroponics.

Classes Are Fun

We had fun in class. In ceramics, Isobel said we made entirely too much noise. We laughed when someone modeled a life-size head resembling some unidentified animal—under pretense of working the clay. Throwing on the potter's wheel is not as easy as Isobel made it look. It was fun when you accidentally put a finger through the side of a very special bowl. Modeling is not so new—a camel looks more "camelish," a dog more "doggish," a coil bowl more like a bowl, and a crumb dish looks more "crummy." The clay is from Iowa. Leanore believes creativity gets us to do something "outside of ourselves."

In Spanish class, Fran had David stand on his head to count up to ten and then back down to one.

I remember fun experiments in senior physics with Kent. How far ***"as the crow flies?"*** We measured the distance to the farm by knowing the speed of sound.

In 2012, six of us had a reunion at the Standing's farm in Earlham, Iowa. We recalled an amusing incident in Freshman Social Science. John fell asleep in class and started to snore. Emily got a class of water and poured it on his head. John told us that he had gotten back to school very late the night previously.

We also had this disgusting project in biology. We had to dissect a small pig. No amount of protest saved us, and the postmortem began. The pig had died of an unknown cause. We had to find the cause, but without success. But we made good notes. It was a challenge to write while holding the nose. We adjourned quickly to make room for the physics class; they moved to the sweet open air of the shop.

Julie's calf was seven months premature. It was exciting to identify the organs, which would have developed in a full-grown calf, and we marveled at how intricate the animal was. Dissecting frogs means poking around in doubtful substances. We found the liver, the stomach, and the spleen. A very lively discussion about which was the pancreas and which the gall bladder. Once we agreed, we made drawings. Some frogs refused to be the exact way the textbook diagrams showed.

Our Very Gifted Faculty Teach Many Courses

Scattergood has a gifted faculty with many skills. Frederick Karl teaches drawing and painting twice a week while pastel and water colors meet on the third day. He shows how Giotto and Rembrandt reflected Brahmanism and Byzantine culture. Frederick also teaches first year Spanish and basic German to three seniors. Isobel Karl teaches ceramics. Robert Berquist has world history for freshmen, government for juniors and seniors, Quakerism for juniors, and the Prophets for seniors.

Kent Erickson teaches math for freshmen, algebra for sophomores, geometry for a combined class of juniors and seniors, and physics for seniors. Harold Burnham teaches science 1 for freshman, biology for juniors, and the life of Paul for freshmen and sophomores.

Joan Erickson teaches sophomore English, and English literature for combined juniors and seniors. Marjorie Catt teaches nutrition and sewing for sophomores in homemaking. I treasured a shirt I had made on a treadle sewing machine years. Class members planned nutritious meals and supervised the kitchen on Saturdays. Agard Bailey has first year Spanish for freshman and oversees construction on the shop. Leanore teaches Quakerism, the Prophets, the Synoptic Gospels, and Old Testament.

Very Creative Teachers

Classes are often challenging. Sophomores rummage in history books to find the Japanese secrets of Pearl Harbor. They thumb through the Ms to find a speech by Moody and look for information about frosts and precipitation in 1941 in New Mexico.

No matter the hour, you will find heads bent over *David Copperfield*. With only a few weeks and 900 pages of Dickens to read, the juniors and seniors use every spare minute. The physics class set out to find out about gravity. They drop things out of the attic of the main building. They sit cross-legged at the bottom of the stairs to watch a baseball suspended as a pendulum.

Members of Oriental Civilization and World Government get official-looking brown envelopes in the mail. They study about their chosen countries and write reports. Did you know that in Sweden murderers are sent to mental hospitals for treatment instead of to prison?

English Is Different at Scattergood

English classes differ from public schools. The junior-senior class concentrates on grammar; freshmen and sophomores read Shakespeare, Scott, Homer, Dickens, Coleridge, Eliot, and Stevenson. They cover *A Midsummer Night's Dream*, *The Lady of the Lake*, *Ivanhoe*, *The Odyssey*, *A Tale of Two Cities*, *Rhyme of the Ancient Mariner*, *Silas Mariner*, *Treasure Island*, and *The Oregon Trail*. Freshmen memorize poetry and write compositions. Sophomores write character sketches, short stories, and letters. Both classes have spelling and vocabulary

The junior-senior English covers biography, drama, and poetry, with emphasis on novels and essays. A great achievement is an autobiography by each junior and senior for class discussion. When they studied the Romantic period, half read biographies of the authors and half wrote research papers.

Junior-senior English is college level. They get lectures, read the various types of literature, write original compositions, and discuss what they read and wrote. Classes meet three times a week for two periods.

This English program is very popular.

Make Mistakes on Purpose

Junior-senior English students laugh when they deliberately strive to make grammatical errors. After reviewing common mistakes, the best part was writing a paper illustrating the mistakes they had learned to avoid. These included faulty parallelism, dangling participles, failure to use the possessive with the gerund, and illogical parallelism.

Freshmen Draw Treasure Island and Make Nautical Dictionary

Freshman English includes reading *Treasure Island*, and this was usually done with supplemental activities—like making nautical dictionaries. Each person's dictionary had a map of how they thought the Treasure Island looked like. As the story got more exciting, pressure from the students forced

Joan to let us read the story in class time as well as study hall. Then we wrote reactions.

Raising Children: Happiness in Life

"Oh dear," moaned a sophomore. "What do I know about raising children? I don't see why Joan wants us to write a paper on this." But another said, "I think it will be fun. Just think of all the times your parents did something you did not like and you vowed never to do that with your kids. This subject has possibilities."

Other subjects include the following: "The Career I May Follow," "The Things I Consider Necessary for Happiness in Life," and "My Ideal Person."

Paramecia, Amoebas, and Diatoms

In a one-celled biology project, we went to the pond to watch paramecia and amoebas swim around madly and divide by fission. Diatoms have two identical halves but some are oblong, a few rectangular, and all have delicate, semi-transparent interiors.

It was exciting each day to see new types appear and old kinds disappear. We saw hundreds of shapes. Colors range from green to red to brown.

My Heart Skipped a Beat: Blood for Science

"Next," said Dr. Loral to the waiting line of pale jittery victims. The smell of alcohol, a pause—a skipped heart beat—and it was all over. Thus it went with twenty-seven victims who gave a few drops of blood for the freshman science and senior biology classes to learn blood testing.

The courageous volunteers and the serums donated by the University Hospital Blood Bank were crucial. Anyone who wished found out their blood type and Rh factor.

Squawking, a Thump, and Wild Flapping

"What are we doing today, Marge?"

"Chickens," said Marge ever so pleasantly.

I had never had any ambition to clean a chicken, but I had much ambition *not to*. There was always that sudden loud squawking, a thump, abrupt silence, and a wild flapping of wings. A door would burst open, the body is plunged into a steaming kettle, and all is quiet.

Marge laughed as she noted our faces with expectancy, curiosity, nervous apprehension, and even undisguised delight. I gathered my courage, grabbed two legs, and rinsed the corpse in cold water. That wasn't so bad.

Sophomores on three mornings each dressed one hen for a total of thirty. They canned 2,000 quarts of tomatoes and tomato juice with the help of faculty and some startled but willing guests. They learned about wool by watching the annual sheep shearing.

Sophomores Can Fruit, Supervise the Kitchen, and Make Cheese Not So Well

Sophomore homemaking class studied fruit and vegetable canning. We canned tomatoes and sweet potatoes in glass jars and prepared peaches and beans for the locker. Each member made two quarts of plum jelly. Three things are needed for cheese—milk, a cheese press, and patience. Sometimes the cheese turned out well, sometimes not so well. What do we have today: George's crummy cheese, Harris's soggy cheese, or Cates's sponge rubber?

We made economical and nutritious meals. Our class oversaw all noon meals. Each Monday a different student took the place of Marge to plan meals and oversee the dining room. Marge did our crew jobs.

We learned whole grains, cereal products, and baking. We followed directions and make exact measures of ingredients.

Southern vs. Northern Wedding Cake: Trilobites in the Cambrian

How does a southern wedding cake differ from a northern cake? One of twenty-five questions for sophomore library research.

Could you find trilobites in the Cambrian? Where can I get advice to clean soiled plumage? We examine the card catalogue, college bulletins, the almanac, readers' guides, encyclopedias, the dictionary of synonyms, the Code of Iowa, and Vogue's Book of Etiquette. A game of hide and seek, but you are always the "It."

Gabriel Sounds the Trumpet to the Farm

Intent physics students listen to the "sound." Why this noise? Physics class discovers wavelengths and frequencies of certain sounds. By holding a receiver before an amplifier and gradually pushing it nearer or farther from the sound, we could hear different tones. At times, the same tone emerged at different points, supposedly equal distances from each other. This even wavelength divided into the speed of sound (1,000 feet per second) produced the frequency of vibrations per minute of this tone.

With our knowledge of the speed of sound tucked away, Kent devised a scheme to measure the distance to the farm. One cold morning, we dismantled several telephone receivers and hitched the bared receivers to the telephone wires at the farm. On campus, several of us shivered, holding with one hand a receiver to our ear and with the other a stopwatch. At the farm, Kent played a trumpet into a telephone, the sound waves first being heard through our receiver. Upon hearing this, someone started the stopwatch, continuing until the sound was heard through the air. After several attempts, we averaged out the time taken for the sound to reach us through the air, thus estimating the distance to the farm.

Disruption Everywhere. Yes, Physics Class!

There was a commotion in the hall as the physics class threw weights at chandeliers, shot lead pencils at falling objects, and tore pianos apart to study the inside. A dishpan full of water contained a bell jar attached to thirty feet of garden hose, attached to an exhaust valve. As the hose was carried down the stairs, the pressure in the bell jar became equal to pressure of the atmosphere minus the pressure of the column of water. By catching and measuring the amount of water overflow, they discovered how the volume of air in the bell jar changes as the pressure in the bell jar changes.

Playing Marbles

What fun! Games in physics. A pair of seniors squat at the end of a long plank—one end was on the rung of a chair to slant while the students roll a marble. What? The teacher allows this in the middle of class. They were timing the descent down an inclined plane.

Another pair shot a marble from a homemade catapult. They want to make the marble hit the same place each time. They have carbon paper over a blank paper on the floor so that it would mark just where it hit. They tried to convince me they were finding the initial horizontal velocity and the final vertical velocity of the marble.

Another a baseball suspended as a pendulum. They recorded measurements of the decreasing swing of the baseball over time to calculate effects of friction.

The last pair to enjoy themselves played catch with one leaning out the attic window and the other below on the ground. On the count of three, the top one dropped a rubber ball, which the bottom one always missed. The bottom person must not have been very sporting because a can on the end of a string always had to be lowered to hoist the ball back up again. The main function of the person on the ground seemed to be to shout some number like "1.6 seconds." They claimed they were timing the fall of a free-falling body in order to determine the acceleration and that 1.6 was the time in seconds. They concluded that the acceleration of gravity is 980 centimeters per second per second. I think they were just making excuses for their strange behavior.

Drosophila, Protozoa, Paramecium, Small Frogs, and Caterpillars

Biology class experiments with drosophila flies to see genetic traits. For the microscope, they are anesthetized and kept in a bottle with cornmeal. Protozoa have amazing shapes. Paramecium races around at high speed. A terrarium with moss, rocks, and ferns has a hibernating toad and several small frogs dug in for winter. We test caterpillars to see if they can move in a straight line between electrically charged wires. A few cocoons for the winter are safe from any "electric fences."

Scattergood Day Presentations

After the Scripture reading, junior biology students report on experiments with fruit flies. Senior physics calls on Albert Einstein and Isaac Newton. Freshmen science explains "the tropisms of seeds." Sophomore homemaking moves the kitchen to the Social Room to show two methods of making a cake. A short skit in Spanish is easily understood by everyone. There is a report on sheep, and an original story from the writing group. Kenichi shows the origin of Japanese characters with a fine brush. Oriental Civilization class tells about China, Japan, and India. They show a map of Japan topography, resources and industries bordered with pictures. Latin class shows the Latin origins of words from Wordsworth's "Tintern Abbey." A pantomime of Casey at the Bat is the end.

With 123 people for lunch, the library served as overflow. Everyone was invited to join one soccer game before lunch and another after.

District Court Is Real Life

The junior-senior government class went to Tipton District Court. A plaintiff was suing for damages from a highway accident. The plaintiff got damages for half the claim of $12,500. J. C. Coonrad, the Clerk of the Court, visited class to answer questions.

Welding Class in West Branch

Harvey Marshall, farm manager, Agard Bailey, shop teacher, and two Scattergood students attended a welding class in the High School Agriculture Building in West Branch. West Branch High sponsors the class for farmers. Frank Elliott, the instructor, gave us two books for the Scattergood library.

Speed Reading

We had films and tests for speed reading. The film starts at 250 words per minute, and thirteen films later, we read at 480 words. Two class periods a week and a test on comprehension at the end.

Freshmen Weather Forecasters

Freshman are up in the clouds to collect data for twenty-four hours. The object on the roof of the boys' dormitory is not a television antenna but a wind vane. A wet and dry bulb table in a book. Two thermometers swung in the air are a hygrometer. Yesterday's Iowa weather map is clipped once a day. The barometer and temperature readings are recorded twice a day. After the class discusses this information, they make a forecast.

They learn clouds from cirrus to cirrostratus to cumulus to nimbus. The sequence helps predict storms. It usually begins with a cirrostratus veil with a milky appearance. Halos indicate moisture. The stratus is next and then nimbostratus—rain clouds. When the storm is nearly over, clouds get dappled and broken—fractostratus. Fair weather comes with billowy castle-like cumulus clouds.

The Scattergood: A Laboratory

In getting out *The Scattergood*, the editor gets assistance in English mechanics with endlessly patient Bob Berquist. "Students make great efforts to improve writing, typing, and printing." The paper suffers from so many learning, but it is valuable experience. Marvelous stories of school events and attitudes for parents, alumnae and other readers.

The editor says, "One thing I learned was that the paper staff have a more sensitive nose for news than one little editor. Thanks is due to all who share so cooperatively in the work and problems." The sophomore English class edited an issue of *The Scattergood* to learn the challenges and get a keener ambition to share in this beacon of news and creative imagination

El Salvador, Korea, Yemen

Once a week, Collection is World Geography. Don led through the capitals and topography of eight Central American countries. El Salvador grows coffee and is the smallest. Costa Rica is the new home of a group of American Quakers with a cheese plant. Harold made a jig-saw puzzle of the countries of South Africa. Bob reported on Korea, which means "Morning Calm." This small country has been under foreign rule since 1904. Its ancient, beautiful culture is being destroyed by war. Joan showed the countries and capitals of the Near East on a movie screen. Did you know the three independent states on the southern coast of Saudi Arabia are Aden, Oman, and Yemen? Frederick showed the cities, topography, and geography of Italy.

Capitalism vs. Communism Brainwashing

Junior-senior government report on articles from news magazines each week. Miriam reported on "brainwashing" from the Christian Century—a person gets "educated" to admit that communism is the right philosophy and that capitalism breeds exploitation and wealth for the minority.

We can ask whether we can answer truthfully that none of the people in this country are exploited, especially those who have to make their living through menial jobs.

No Letter Grades

I went to both grade school and Scattergood with no letter grades. Reports, however, always suggest that we can do better if we apply ourselves. My Geometry teacher wrote, "There is no point in turning in shoddy work like this as you will just have to do it over again." One report said, "Walton improves on keeping a neat room, but still has a much room for improvement." My great organization, however, of having in my archive the letters written by my parents in the nineteen-fifties is great.

Four Parties Vote for President

While the rest of the world watched the presidential candidates, Scattergood held a mock election. Several weeks before Scattergood election day—November 3, 1952—signs appeared on doors and bulletin boards: "How does your candidate propose to obtain peace?" "Can we cooperate with Russia?" and "Can you lead your party and not be led by it?"

The government class organized the campaign and election by dividing into groups to support Democrats, Republicans, Socialists, and Progressives, with undecided as "Independents." Two Friday night Collections were devoted to comparing parties for the benefit of the undecided. The arguments are very convincing—we wished we had more than one vote.

One hundred percent participation, with absentee ballots for those away from school. On Monday, Democrats, 19; Socialists, 15; Republicans, 13; and Progressives, 11. We stayed up to hear the returns on the radio.

We Assisted West Branch Elections

In November 1952, members of the Scattergood community of the age twenty-one or older went to vote in West Branch. Three Government students folded ballots and told of their experiences.

A Quaker Look at Platforms

Junior-senior government class went to West Branch to hear Dr. Manfred Kuhn of the University of Iowa on "A Quaker Looks as the Platforms."

We Get *International Conciliation*

We now subscribe to *International Conciliation* from Carnegie Endowment for International Peace.

What Is Important?

"What is important to you as an individual? I do not mean what do you think ought to be important to you, but what really is?" The staff thought it more important than classes to discuss what we want out of life.

We begin with ten minutes of silence. All our needs boil down to security. We want security in material ways, in our beliefs, in our goals, in our knowledge of ourselves, and in fellowship with others.

At four o'clock, the boys went camping. The freshmen and juniors bike to Todd's Park and the sophomores and seniors to Millett's Pasture. The girls carried on at school with great enjoyment.

The next morning, we continued. For security, we must have purposeful work, food and shelter, knowledge, and of self-expression in the arts. To bring world peace, we must start with our own community and work up through larger and larger groups. To make our community ideal, we must all share responsibility and work. We discuss griping, its effects upon community, and what to do about it. At Scattergood, we learned what we will find in few other places.

Before lunch, several told what the conference had meant. It got our thinking apparatus in motion and gave a push in the right direction.

Graduates at Twenty-Three Widely Scattered Colleges

Scattergood graduates are at Earlham, Friends University, Wilmington, Tennessee Polytechnic Institute, Blackburn, Heidelberg, University of

Iowa, Grandview, Harvard, Montgomery Junior College, Whittier, Penn, U. of Minnesota, Waldorf, Manchester, Bluffton, Iowa State, University of South Dakota, Drake, Occidental, Haverford, North East Missouri State, and Radcliffe.

Sophomore Book Fair Huge Success

The Sophomore class sponsored a Book Fair. They selected 200 children's books and made posters to spread about West Branch. It was publicized in the *West Branch Times*. The Municipal Hall was decorated with posters. On tables along with the books were figures made of paper-mache by art students.

R. F. Hodomann, Superintendent of the West Branch Schools, had classes visit the fair. Sophomores gave a pantomime of the "Golden Goose" with piano accompaniment by Don Harris. They reviewed books for each grade. Students looked at the displays, and many returned the next day to place orders. Sophomores read aloud to younger students.

On the last day, Scattergood students and the community attended another presentation of "The Golden Goose," followed by a talk by Ruth Wagner of the Iowa Pupils Reading Circle. She told how books play a part in the lives of children and mentioned several books and authors. People browsed and left orders.

Eighty books, fifty different titles, were sold and brought in $172. After expenses, $30 remained for books for the Scattergood Library.

Campaigns Up Close

Eight members of the Berquist junior-senior government class went to Tipton to hear Governor Beardsley and Representative Thomas Martin give campaign speeches.

Soil Conservation and Bud Grafting

In freshman science, we learned soil conservation. There were rave reviews from graduates later. Buildings and grounds crew grafted buds on fruit trees, which today feed the school.

Holiday Music

With the holidays coming, small books of carols are passed out in Collection. Four groups learn soprano, alto, tenor, and base. Our repertoire includes less well-known songs. We sing carols in the hall before supper.

Freshmen See Pyramus and Thisbe

Freshman English reads Shakespeare's *Midsummer Night's Dream* and attends "Pyramus and Thisbe" by a high school group in Iowa City.

Shop Classes Excited about New Tools

The shop class painted the dining room. They set up new power and hand tools, including a circular saw, jig saw, drill press, jointer, and lathe. New hand tools are wrenches, drills, many of bits, several hammers, a rip saw, and wood and metal vices. Two new work benches were constructed. Four old work benches from the 1920s came out of storage. An arc welder, now sitting forlornly in the laundry addition, will be used for welding class next year.

Some Want Extra Quiet

Evening study hall is rearranged for students who want an especially quiet study hall to use the library or math room. Wow, it was amazing how serious and really quiet we were.

3

We Find Beauty around Us

Deer Tracks on My Window

WHEN MY WINDOWS FROST, they become ivory carved walls in my palace of dreams. I see penguins tobogganing on their stomachs at the frigid South Pole. I think of deer tracks in the snow and of how bewildered a rabbit would feel on a clean smooth sheet of ice, trying to jauntily hop along, but skidding and sliding instead.

Occasionally the frost patterns make me think of the grotesque yet graceful forms of the barren winter trees or a fantastic masterpiece of modern art. But then my newly acquired wallpaper gives way to wet window panes, as though wiping away all dreams of fantasy.

Juncos, Chickadees, Horned Larks, Longspurs, and Tree Sparrows

When Old Man Winter blows down from the north, bringing the cold, the ice, and snow, we find much of nature is dormant: trees have lost their leaves, plant life has become dormant, and the birds have left for their southern abodes.

At this time of year, from the distant Arctic come birds who find the frosty air and sparkling snow quite suited to their habits and happiness. The plain but handsome juncos, in their stately jackets of gray, come in abundance and fill the air wherever they are with their happy twitter. Horned Larks fly over the snow-bound fields, singing their high tinkling melodies in spite of the icy winds. The red-capped tree sparrows frolic in the barren trees and shrubbery. Occasionally we see a flock of longspurs, with their black crowns, and even snow buntings.

Some birds have been with us during the summer but are brave enough to endure the cold. The chickadees, in black cap and black bib, merrily frisk from branch to branch, from tree to tree, upside down much of the time, calling to the world in their pleasing *chickadee-dee-dee*. From the top of some evergreen, we apt to hear a titmouse, who, though dressed in gray, carries a snowy crest on his head and cheers the world with his ringing whistle. Looking at the trunk of a tree, we might find quite an acrobat, the little nuthatch, who walks up and down the trunks of many trees in search of insects emitting his sweet nasal call. The cardinal, in a fine red coat and crest, during the cold weather reminds us that spring is ahead, in his loud, clear whistle. The noisy blue jays add color and life in the winter scene.

A list of winter friends includes juncos, horned larks, red-capped tree sparrows, an occasional flock of longspurs with black crowns, and snow buntings. Summer and winter chickadees are amusing to watch as they go upside down much of the time. We hear a titmouse and a nuthatch walks up and down in search of insects with a sweet call. Their happiness and cheerfulness remind us that the world is not completely dead but is still full of vigor and gladness and that we may enjoy it.

4

Camping Is Exciting

CAMPING IS THE MOST eagerly awaited event each spring and fall at Scattergood. Inevitably "there are ashes in the pancakes" and "we get home tired but happy." Getting back and forth to the campsite is a great adventure. Spooky stories, singing around the campfire, collecting burrs on socks, falling into the creek, or shivering in sleeping bags just add to the experience.

Classes Choose Their Outings

For Spring outings the sophomores went to Whittier, the juniors to the woods. The seniors camped at the Palisades on the Cedar River and the freshmen spent a very wet afternoon at Israel's Pasture. The Whittier group picked ten bushels of pears and coated potatoes with mud to cook in the ashes. They sang and told stories before getting cold in their sleeping bags. They were up at five to get warm by the fire and have breakfast.

Off Like a Flash

As soon as that last class was over, I was off like a flash. There were many things to do before setting off into the woods. The bicycle must be put together, the blankets rolled up with extras including a worn out flashlight, raincoat, ear muffs, and gloves. By the time I was ready to leave, the other campers had hit the trail for the river. At the first crossroad, I discovered a low tire but pushed onward to reach camp before dark. As I was trying to enjoy the landscape in the rays of the setting sun, a troop of trucks came tearing by, throwing dust everywhere. About dark, my companion and I almost missed the farm driveway, our last turn. The way back into the woods was rough, and at one point, I thought that either my bicycle would fall apart, or I would.

At camp, we gather wood and collect burrs. For dinner, we get dough to toast bread sticks over the fire. We have potato salad, bacon and eggs, apples, and carrots large enough for Paul Bunyon. I start to sort the bedrolls in the station wagon, but suddenly realize that the moonlight is perfect for a snipe hunt. We get no snipes but have a great escapade.

After a few rusty and a few really good ghost stories, the boys set up camp down the hills and the girls around the campfire. The ground was very wet, so in the morning, we hurried to get close to the campfire. We had until noon to get back to school so we rocked an old tree in the water, hiked around, and gathered specimens of moss and unusual plant life.

On the bicycle trip home, a farmer with a load of corncobs asked me if I was playing hooky. I saw an interesting old house with ancient lightning rods keeping company with a shiny new television antenna and narrow old brick windows with modern venetian blinds. By the time I got back to school I was sweating because I had worn winter clothes for cool nights.

Eight-Mile Bike Trip

Millet's Pasture is peaceful until the junior and senior classes fill the air with chatter. The food arrives by station wagon, so we quickly gather firewood. After the eight-mile bike trip, we are ready to eat plenty of bread twists, potato salad, eggs and bacon, and carrot sticks. Then we have singing and storytelling around the campfire.

We each get a huge slice of watermelon given to us during a trip to Coneseville to glean sweet potatoes. The boys went down the pasture from the campfire, and we all settled down for a cold night. After a breakfast of pancakes, we spent the morning exploring, and collecting burrs on socks. We arrived home just in time for lunch.

Flavored with Ashes

Spring and fall camping are always eagerly anticipated. Fourteen miles on balloon tires, no gears, over hilly gravel roads to Israel's pasture is no big challenge for a teenager. By dark, supper is ready at the campfire. We know many folk songs and enjoy the harmonica accompaniment. We just expect a breakfast flavored with ashes. A spoke-like formation around the campfire gives equal warmth to all. Spooky ghost stories keep us from wandering off in the dark. After shivering in our bedrolls all night, we are glad for a hot fire in the morning. Exploring parties set out in all directions and look at rundown houses. We run from too friendly horses and pick hard pears and wild apples. We return to campus with watery eyes and smelling like smoke. At Lake

McBride, the campers had observed singing frogs by flashlight, seemingly unaware of being observed. Listening to the frog chorus under the stars was an unforgettable experience. We had great fellowship as we gathered wood for the campfire and fixed meals.

Telltale Heart Chills

After trudging up hill and downhill for a full mile and a half with sleeping bags, food, and heaviest thing of all, a six-gallon milk can of water, the sophomores reached the middle of Israel's Pasture. We waited for the more energetic ones who had made the fourteen-mile trip on bikes.

After a little rest, we all gather firewood, but the matches were missing. Two went back the mile to a farmhouse and returned with matches. We played hide and seek. Harold sent chills up our spines with Poe's "Telltale Heart" and "The Black Cat."

We report breakfast flavored with ashes and return to school very tired but happy.

Raw in the Middle

On a bright sunny day, the freshmen and seniors went camping. To get to Israel's Pasture, we seniors squeezed into the station wagon with sleeping bags and food. When we arrived, we found an extra pan of cake, so Marj went off to deliver it the freshmen.

Dinner was a huge success. Raw-in-the-middle bread twists and sizzling wieners never tasted so good. A roaring campfire was a soothing background to Agard's tales of prison life. We rolled into our sleeping bags under a clear sky but woke up when bucket-sized rain drops began drumming a rhythm that made our feet dance—in a bee-line to the station wagon. Pixie got there first in spite of her short legs. She started climbing over the front seat but then gasped: "Someone is in here." At that, Rolland raised a sleepy hand and grumbled something about intruding on a person's bedroom. Before he could voice his complete opinion, we all had oozed in for the night.

The next day, after a three o'clock snack in the kitchen, the senior class climbed into dry beds. It was a trip we will always remember.

Beans Shoot Up in the Air

Sweet potatoes sizzle in the pan. Cans of beans are in the coals. Carrots are sliced. Some tell stories around the fire and others look for sleeping sites. Suddenly there was a huge pop and beans shoot up from the fire. Holes had not been punched in the bean cans. We remove them with sticks and splatter ashes into the potatoes. But that was not a problem as we are camping. We twist dough around sticks for roasting over the coals. Many are dark black on the exterior with raw dough in the middle. A few done slowly are perfect. No matter the quality, they were spread with jelly and eaten with enthusiasm. Our potatoes are partially done, and the beans are warm. We sing and tell stories around the campfire. Most manage to sleep well, thanks to those who added wood to the fire in the middle of the night.

Wild Cat Steak on a Stick

"If there are now six seniors, thirteen juniors, several faculty, Howard and Reva Hampton, and camping utensils and food in the bus, we are ready to leave." Then one of Howard Hampton's big highway buses, with waving arms extended from the windows, moved out in the direction of the Mississippi River.

The bus was too heavy to cross one of the old bridges, so we unloaded just across the stream from our camp site in Wild Cat Den State Park. The senior homemaking class started preparing the meal as soon as adequate, as well as inadequate, fires had been started. Each of three meal prep groups had invited several victims to share supper, including wild cat steak (wild cat steak is a meat and onion mix, wrapped on a stick and roasted over a fire somewhere in Wild Cat Den State Park) and chocolate cake.

After supper, several people took a cool walk along the stream and returned with their clothes soaked from walking in dewy grass, and trying to cross a stream by building stepping stones.

Around the campfire, we listened to a long poem about Sam McGee, recited by Earl George. Don Harris sang "Ole Man River," and we unrolled our bedrolls under a clear night sky and looked for favorite constellations.

At five in the morning, the whiskers of a friendly deer woke Leanore Goodnow. After breakfast, the park custodian opened the ancient, three-story mill to our inspection. We spent the rest of the morning climbing the rocks and examining the wild cat dens near the picnic area.

Weird Screams and Frost on the Face

"Arise, woods dwellers! Prepare to defend yourselves. The juniors and seniors are coming!" We heard this warning as half of Scattergood descended on the Palisades-Kepler State Park near Mount Vernon on one of the coolest afternoons in September.

We did the usual things: followed trails along the river, took pictures, and tried very hard to get lost. One carload who had been picking apples in Whittier arrived late but explored the woods and walked by the river before stew and bread rolls around the fire. A few tried roasting apples or frying tomatoes. When there were dishes to do, all but a few mysteriously disappeared.

We all came back when the woods got chilly to the dubious comfort of a tiny fire, a folksong fest, and a long and involved fairytale by Walt. We went to bed, some to warmth and sleep and a few to a night of icy toes and checking out the constellations.

During the night, we heard weird screams. We disputed whether it was a crow or a cougar. If a cougar, we assumed it was not hungry. Everyone gathered for a pancake breakfast. Several had stiff necks, icy toes, and frost on their faces. A brisk hike down to the Cedar River, to see the mists rise and the moon set, warmed us up.

Pop Corn, Ghost, and the Missing Miniature

Our entire junior class, yes, all five of us, were sitting together during lunch when Leanore announced camping trips. We were very excited, and as soon as Harold and Nance joined us at the table, we made final plans.

At 2:30, we met in the dining room, confronted by a table full of equipment. We were almost ready to leave, but we hesitated as it was raining. We sat in our camping clothes while the rain came pattering down, trying to think of a solution. One foolish soul playfully suggested using the newly built hog houses for shelter, and before we knew it, we were off to the farm. That plan was abandoned when we found they were already occupied, and the occupants did not extend a very hearty welcome.

By this time, however, the rain had ceased, and by unanimous decision, we were off to the woods. More equipment was gathered to be prepared for more rain. Supplies were now seven sleeping bags, food for one meal, dishes, two skillets, several tarpaulins, ukulele, and rain coats.

We left at four with the equipment packed on our backs. We seven must have looked odd, trudging through the mud and stray drops of rain—especially to the West Branch school bus driver who passed us several times.

We reached the South Woods, three miles from school at 5:45. A beautiful secluded spot, far away from civilization (although we could hear the cars on the road) and just the right size for our group.

The spot was soon a beehive of activities. Two went to a farmhouse for water, the fire was built, and a tarpaulin put up. Soon the potatoes were frying, beefsteak was sizzling, biscuit batter was fried, and corn was heating. We sat round the campfire and sang to the accompaniment of the uke. One ambitious member popped some popcorn, and as we munched it, we played several rounds of Ghost.

When the yawns started and the campfire began to die we unrolled the sleeping bags. Harold read several chapters from *The Missing Miniature*. One went to sleep during the first chapter, one during the second, and . . .

We were up at 5:15 and marched toward home. Before we had gone more than a mile, the station wagon came. We protested the humiliation but secretly were glad.

5

Collection

COLLECTION IS A SPECIAL time when the whole school gathers for thirty minutes before bedtime, except on Thursday when boys and girls have house meetings. We have a large variety of intellectual and cultural experiences.

Last Bell Is Collection

The last bell at 8:30 is evening Collection at. We gather in the Social Room to discuss community problems or listen to a selection from our large collection of classical records. A Collection committee arranges programs. Students select music for the Friday nights that we do not have a story. The story of Beethoven and the creation of a symphony was a profound experience. Sometimes song books are passed out. The singing group sang one evening, and once the girls taught songs to the boys. Classes prepare skits and educational programs. Faculty members give quizzes on world geography lessons.

On Sunday night, we plan Monday's work projects such as picking up apples from the ground, gleaning potatoes, cleaning up the campus, or cleaning up the farm woodlot. On Mondays, a different student each week reads the Log—sheep getting into the cornfields gets a laugh. We learn how to conduct business according to Friends' principles, with a different student clerk each week. We have visitors from a variety of businesses and professions telling about their hobbies, jobs, trips, life experiences and their daily lives, and prominent Quakers discuss political and social problems.

Harold Burnham reported on the World Conference of Young Friends and Oxford Friends World Conference in England. On Thursday, each dorm has a house meeting. A special treat is Leanore reading *Winnie the Pooh* and *The Little Flowers of St Francis*. The gentle humor and philosophy of Pooh are congenial with Quaker values. Leanore also reads from *Green Pastures*, *Alice in Wonderland*, and *The Friendly Persuasion* by Jessamyn West about Indiana Quakers during the Civil War. *I Remember Mama* tells about a Norwegian family in San Francisco. She gives lively accounts of her activities away from school. We close each evening with quiet meditation. On Saturday nights, we have basketball, parties, folk dancing, and movies.

A report tells that Ellis and Walt were the winners of a cow judging contest organized by Frank Bedell. The walk a half mile up to Yankee Corner each Sunday evening is a chance for bashful young fellows to hold hands with a date.

Edward Bear Gently Entertains

Hunny is famous on campus. We learned from Edward Bear, or Winnie the Pooh, that it is desirable to have a little something to settle that eleven o'clock feeling. The little something is always hunny. "Oh help, Bother," Pooh has worked his head into jar of hunny, but we are glad to have him visit Collection. We enjoy stories about Hefalump hunts, lost tails, birthday parties, and the wisdom of Christopher Robin. We meet Piglet, Eyore, Owl, Tigger, Rabbit, and all who live in the Hundred Acre Wood. Pooh always stops in the middle of the most exciting action for "just a little something."

To please Edward Bear, three bee hives arrived on a platform behind the gym to be managed by Frederick Karl with help from Bryan Paul Michener and Danny Neifert, who did a presentation on bee-keeping. We are glad to have a superior kind of sweetener than refined sugar.

Girls Learn to Conduct House meetings

Once a week, the boys and girls meet separately in house meetings to discuss issues of dormitory life. The girls formalized their conduct of business. The group is called to order by a chairman who asks for the reading of the previous week's minutes. Old and new business follow. Faulty plumbing, noisy early risers, and lights left on unnecessarily are typical problems. We aim to complete the business in as short a time as possible in order to have social time.

The meetings are held in a different room each week, and the occupants provide entertainment. One room taught a new game, and on another night, we listened to a James Thurber story. Recently we began reading aloud *My Dear Ego* by Fritz Kunkel.

Benetta Tells of Bike Trip in Europe with Jenifer

Benetta Morgan gave an account of a summer trek by bicycle through Europe with her sister, Jenifer. From Oxford, England, they bicycled north to Lincoln and York, taking in the Yorkshire moors.

They met many interesting people while getting inexpensive lodging at youth hostels. From the hilly part of England, they cycled to Glasgow, Scotland, visited Loch Lomond and Loch Katrine, and moved on through Sterling, Dunbar, and Edinborough, and then returned to Harwich, England, to take the boat to Denmark. They rode over the brightly colored countryside to Hamburg and followed the River Lahn to its union with the Rhine. From Cologne, they rode a freight barge to Amsterdam. After a trip through Belgium, they sailed from Calais to Dover. During all of their touring, they found the young people eager to talk despite the language barriers.

Footsie with the Reds

On October 22, 1951, Jerome Davis spoke. He supervised prisoner of war work in twenty-nine camps in Czarist Russia and was the first American to work with Russian soldiers under the Czar. He was in charge of all YMCA war work in Russia and remained there throughout the revolution.

He was the first American to interview Stalin. He thinks the Russians have a standard of living slightly below the English. He visited Russia in 1943 and traveled 10,000 miles. His dispatches appeared in American and foreign newspapers.

The commander of the Iowa American Legion, of West Branch, accused the school of "playing footsie with the Reds." Several newspaper editors took exception to his remarks and his statement "Leanore received one of the greatest compliments of her tenure during this episode—communicated by silence." No one called, and no one wrote.

Historic Christian Leaders

In pre-meeting Collection each First Day, a faculty member presents the life and writings of a religious leader. First was Thomas à Kempis, whose *On the Imitation of Christ* we have been listening to as morning devotions after breakfast. Next were Christian leaders back to the beginnings of Christianity, and St. Augustine, St. Patrick, and St. Benedict. Frederick Karl, who had studied in a Jesuit school in Europe, told us about Ignatius Loyola, the progressive and intelligent founder of the Society of Jesus. Other leaders were John Wesley, William Booth, Jean Calvin, and Leo Tolstoy.

6

The School Committee

The School Committee Is Extremely Dedicated

THE SCHOOL COMMITTEE OF the Iowa Yearly Meeting of Friends (Conservative) functions as a board of directors for the school.

They met Saturday, February 3, 1951. In spite of the cold weather, seventeen members were present. Four sent excuses. The next meeting is June 9 with subcommittees meeting in March and April.

Consideration was given to the faculty for next year, which will remain substantially the same so far as can now be determined.

Members of the Committee from Paullina brought fifty gallons of corn and a dozen kitchen aprons. The continuing contributions to the food supply at the school was stressed. The school is very much in need of lard for the remainder of the year, and some contributions of lard were promised.

The Farm Committee met to consider progress at the farm, and to plan a day of wood-sawing. This will supplement fuel at school.

Students had lunch with Committee members.

Deputations went to meetings in Whittier, West Branch, Ackworth, Bear Creek, Paullina, and Stavanger to discuss plans for a new dormitory.

New Dormitory

We were unsuspecting as we gathered in the Social Room for evening Collection. The School Committee had spent the day with us as they do a number of times each year. Those of us fortunate enough to have parents attend the Committee meeting are happy to get an occasional glimpse of Mother or Dad, but we had no idea that they were keeping a secret. When Leanore said the Committee came together to consider the gift of a new boys' dorm, we were floored.

Sixty-five thousand dollars for a new boys' dormitory is from a foundation set up to aid educational projects. The Committee unanimously accepted the gift and approved the plans. Construction will begin as soon as weather permits, and the due date for completion is August 25.

Henry Fisk of Iowa City is the architect. The building will be similar to the Instruction Building. The building will be two stories in addition to a basement, so it will not be suitable as a student project. Floyd Fawcett and Howard Hampton have met with an architect from the foundation who will review the plans.

Fireproof construction for safety since boys sleep through bells and sirens. It will have living quarters for a married counselor. The present boys' dormitory will serve as faculty family, sick isolation, and attic storage.

This unit will bring to a close the immediate building program as the most urgent needs of the school will have been met.

7

Community Life

FUNDAMENTAL VALUES OF SCATTERGOOD are community and cooperation. In the work program, students and staff serve the School Community by cooperation in building construction, farm work, maintenance, and many routine tasks. Most of the students, directly or indirectly, help with meals every day.

Change Table Seating Every Three Weeks

We sit with the same people for meals for a three-week period. We learn how to wait tables and perform the duties of host.

Tables change the day following shifts in crew jobs. We are assigned seats by student committee. Seating positions are recorded on a large scroll of brown paper over four feet long. A staff member constitutes a sixth member, and each table has a mix of grade levels. We come to know our schoolmates well and keep in touch for decade after graduation.

Get Your Stuff Off My Bed

Changing beds is test of character when roommates change.

"This is my bed, where's yours?"

"Hey, get your stuff off my bed. It's mine now."

"What a mess!"

"Look out, I'm coming through."

Learning to live close together requires patience and forbearance.

Faculty Kids Howl, Squirm, Gurgle, Stare, Bubble, and Leanore Hovers

I wandered into the Social Room and found the faculty children assembled. There was restrained excitement in the air. On one couch Sara Berquist sits holding Paul, age four months, who stares about in bored manner. Beside her is Barbara Henderson making brave efforts to keep Jerry, six months, from squirming away. A very grown-up David Laughlin, two and a half years, wanders around, hands clasped behind his back, directing sage looks at the younger and quizzical glances at the older. David's mother, Lois, sits holding Janet, who gurgles and blows bubbles, making noises of a five-month-old. Hovering over first one and then the other is Leanore Goodenow.

The children are to have their pictures taken by Harold, who has not arrived. The children were taken from their naps without being fed and were beginning to fuss. Leanore worried, mothers fidgeted, Janet gurgled, Jerry fussed, and Paul stared.

At last, Harold arrives. He sets up his camera, and the children are deposited on a green couch. Students and parents gather in a semicircle to watch. It is an exciting moment; then Jerry begins to cry. He screams, and he howls. He does not like it and lets us know. Janet refuses to sit up straight and keeps leaning coyly against Paul. David worries with all the noise. Jerry will not be consoled. He quits for a moment, allowing Harold to take a picture, but the flash does not go off. Again Jerry howls, Janet leans, and David worries. Harold tries once more. The camera clicks, the flash flashes, and everyone is happy . . . except Jerry, but he wins after all as the film is blank.

Betty Jo attempted to take a picture of David while he was helping with the garden hose, but he was self-conscious, and Betty Jo received a shower.

Campus Children Are Fun

Children on campus are entirely unpredictable and fun. Muriel had her first birthday cake and enjoyed her "Happy Birthday" serenade. She has a smile for everybody and loves to tell stories in an unknown language.

Little Isabel gets out for a walk with Mamma or for a sled ride in her basket. Instead of crying when we talk to her, she is beginning to talk back. We have to be careful what we say to Paul Berquist since he is apt to say the very same thing back. Bob Berquist, his papa, said in his presence: "Paul is a little dickens." Now Paul takes joy in saying, "Paul is dickens," pronouncing every word very clearly.

When Paul Berquist arrived, there were three other children under six months. "Our contacts with these very young members of the community make a pleasant variation in our lives."

Leanore Had Professional Photographs Taken of Each Class, the Faculty, and the Whole School

Leanore was wonderful about getting professional class and school photographs, and Douglas Parker took a lot of wonderful Kodachrome slides.

Harold Burnham took many shots of the seniors in 1950, specifically of Tom Blackburn and Muriel Mott and Lora Beth Henderson smirking for the camera. A special one was of Earl George peering up from deep in the septic tank of the boys' dormitory with a bucket, smudges of sludge all over his face.

Informal class photographs are treasures. One shows the freshman of the class of 1953 in front of the office with members standing, leaning, or kneeling and petting three lambs. A faculty photo has Bob Berquist with his hands in a prayer-like pose admiring a faculty baby. Each year, community members display photos, and we sign up for copies. These capture many phases of campus life, especially work crews.

Junior and Senior Boys Carve Roast Chicken

On Thanksgiving, the junior and senior boys were hosts. They carved a roast chicken on each table. We then gathered in the Social Room for a ballad skit with shadow puppets, and slides by Edgar Anderson about the amazing wonders of corn in South America.

Fire Safety and Drill

A fire committee was appointed to check and demonstrate fire equipment. In Collection, they explained five kinds of extinguishers: carbon dioxide, carbon tetrachloride, Pyrene type, bulb carbon tetrachloride, and soda acid. The committee made suggestions to improve fire safety.

Two nights after the presentation, a fire drill was planned, but the siren lever got stuck. When they tried again, the boys gathered in the office in two and a half minutes. It took the girls three and one-quarter minutes to collect in a classroom. The crews at the farm thought it was a real fire and came over to offer assistance. Neighbors came. This was because the previous drills had been at night, and no one ever thought of having one any other time. We learned that the siren should not be run so long on drills. Fire buckets have now been repainted red and filled with sand. The school feels a safer now.

Double Decker Beds

The girls' dormitory is crowded with four girls per room. Closets are jam packed. Double-decker beds give a ceiling-scraper effect.

In All Directions Evening Meal

At an unexpected gathering in the Social Room one First Day afternoon, Leanore explained that we were not having our conventional meal. Groups of four or five were to be formed, including one or two faculty. Each would choose its meal. We checked cook books, put pots and pans put into baskets, and grabbed food.

Students donned jeans and set out for a camp fire meal. A group used the hayloft as a slide. The Laughlin's lawn was a picnic place. Waffles or pancakes made up the menu of those who preferred to eat indoors at the Berquist cottage, Leanore's office, or the Laughlin kitchen. An ambitious group drove to Iowa City for a restaurant meal. We had so much fun that we found it difficult to get back to school for Collection.

8

Crews Keep Scattergood Running

THE MANY CREWS AT Scattergood are essential. They are usually fun and sometimes very memorable, but always create great fellowship. Most of the students, directly or indirectly, help with the meals every day. Farm and garden crews supply the kitchen; and vegetable prep, baking, and meal prep crews prepare food. Pots, pans, and dish crews wash utensils; and the floor mopping crew cleans the kitchen for the next day. Laundry keeps us clean.

Each student has a crew job and assignments change every three weeks. The most heroic job is the chore crew, which goes over to the farm to milk the cows and feed the livestock. After getting up at five in the morning, or sometimes earlier when deep snow slows the trip to the farm, and the temperature is ten below zero, they feel very heroic. They go over again in the afternoon. After their three weeks, they are ready for an easier job.

We Love Our Crew Jobs

The work program is central in campus life. I never heard anyone complain. Chore crew—which was in charge of milking the cows—is only three weeks until new crew assignments. We get to know our schoolmates well in the fellowship and "hi jinks" of vegetable peeling, meal cooking, table setting, doing dishes and pots, gardens and grounds, laundry, and cleaning the dining room.

Tasks such as helping Leanore in the office, stoking the furnaces and hot water heaters, assisting a faculty member on maintenance, or cleaning the bathrooms are more individual. Student work had risks—a hot water heater fire got so hot that steam came out of the cold water tap. Opened faucets let out clouds of steam. Charlie and Dick leaned out windows shouting for help. "London fog" was the joke, but no hot water for showers was not so funny. Some people, seeing the clouds of steam coming out the windows, thought that the dorm was on fire.

Flat Coffee Cake Tastes Just Fine

First Day mornings are special with Wheaties instead of oatmeal, and our famous coffee cake with crunchy brown sugar crust on top. When I got to the kitchen, I found an apron flung on the table, and recipes and cook books strewn about. After consultation with Charlie, the cake went into the oven. Time passed. Several peeps into the oven found the cake browning but with only a couple of rising bubbles showing. The little hills proved to be only air pockets, and the cake was dense and thin. It tasted good, and people ate it. Investigation showed that one of two baking powder cans had mistakenly been filled with flour. Not very good leavening.

A Smelly Critter in the Dark

Chore crews can be very memorable. On a dark morning on the shortcut through the tomato vines and barbed wire, Anne, just ahead of me, stopped and let me pass. Was she just being polite, or . . .

I remarked that I smelled a skunk but thought nothing of the slight rustling beside the gate. The moon was covered with clouds, and it was too dark to see the path. Then I heard Anne, "There it is beside you, Margie!"

I saw a huge raised tail. In a split second, I was twenty feet south.

Shaking, we climbed the fence and made a wide detour. A skunk in daylight is bad, but face-to-face at night is dangerous.

Skating through Water

The kitchen is a beehive after breakfast. Four on vegetable prep peel potatoes, carrots, turnips, kohlrabi, and onions. They wash squash and kale. Two do pots and pans, and the baker mixes dough. A drummer slaps out rhythms on the table; others follow suit, and the room erupts with hand-clapping, stomping, and wiggling to the beat.

When conversation lags, a song breaks out. Putting away peelers, brushes, knives, and pans requires staying upright while skating through water. Even though the onion peelers are mournful with their tears, the fellowship starts the day in a pleasant mood as students go off to classes and study hall. Seven is a fun group. Confusion keeps us on our toes with the baker at one end of the table, vegetable prep at the other end, and pots and pan circulating between the sinks, stove, and shelves. The mop crew leaves the kitchen shining.

Oh, My Aching Back: Worst Crew Ever

Garden crew is in charge of thinning carrots. They begin as tiny feathery sprouts like hairs on a "crew cut." You crouch down to pinch very gingerly to keep from accidentally wiping out hundreds. It is tricky to get the distance between each plant at three inches. Which are best plants to leave? It s hard to get the roots out if you accidentally pull off the tops. It took a lot of time—results were not obvious.

Yes, true carrot lovers hate to discard any carrots. If they are too thick, only a few will be large enough and the rest will rot. We now know why nobody likes carrots as well as I do. It's just that I had never thinned them before. The great reward is rhyming carrot with anything really disgusting. The crew fellowship was great but did not get anyone to love carrots no matter how many vitamins and minerals they have. A wonder carrots ever get to the table.

Take It Off, Begin Again

The building crew's task is to lay blocks. It is much more complicated than it looked. The mortar goes down the holes in the blocks. Unless the mortar pasty enough, it does not stick on the block and takes five or six tries. Leveling the block requires pounding until it looks the right height. If it is too high, you can pound some more, but too low, woe! Take it off, and begin again. Then knock the block so there is only half a horizontal inch between it and the next to sit squarely.

When bubbles on the level are in the middle, just the pointing remains to smooth the mortar into the grooves. "One block will take up the time you are able to spend on building, but try again tomorrow. It's fun." Miriam was very proud of laying just one block because she had to re-do it six times.

9

Culture at Scattergood

FOR A SMALL SCHOOL in rural Iowa, Scattergood has a remarkable variety of music, drama, and guest speakers.

Folk Songs, Hungarian Dances, Brandenburg

Music was prohibited by early Quakers as frivolous and associated with unreputable places like bars. My mother claimed that we went to Scattergood instead of the other Quaker boarding school in Ohio, Olney, because Scattergood had music while Olney did not, though Daddy was on the Olney School Committee.

We knew a lot of folk songs and sang around the campfire on camping trips. I still remember "Sumer Is a Cumin In," "English Country Gardens," and "A Spanish Cavalier" from a Singing Interest Group.

A classmate, Winifred, who had an operatic voice, sang for Collection, "Oh No John, No John, No John No" about a guy who gets the girl by rephrasing the question so that "No" turns out to be "Yes."

No radios were allowed on campus, but we had an extensive phonograph record collection of classical music. Hungarian Dances, Romanian Rhapsodies, and Brandenburg Concertos echoed through the Main Building from the Social Room before supper every evening. Guests taught us folk songs in Collection in foreign languages. Classical records included Shakespeare songs, Debussy, "The Young Person's Guide to the Orchestra" and "La Traviata" by Verdi.

Masters in the Hall, Messiah, Jeanette Isabella

In Pre-Meeting Collection, we listened to Luke's Christmas story and heard the first part of Handel's "Messiah." In the afternoon, the second part was played for those who chose to come. In evening Collection, we heard the third part, "After the Crucifixion."

We had three singing groups, one of girls and two of boys. Anywhere on campus, one would hear

"Masters in the Hall" and "Jeanette, Isabella." The freshmen dramatized "Bird's Christmas Carol." They told Christmas stories, including "A Pinata for Pepita" about a Mexican girl. In Collection, they presented the Christmas Eve adventures of Mole and Rat from "The Wind in the Willows."

The Tipton High School chorus of twelve ushered in Christmas with "Bring a Torch Jeanette, Isabella" and "Bringing in the Boars Head." Then we all sang together. They arrived before dinner, and after we had shown them our dorms, joined informal groups in games. We have been singing carols around the piano, and Collections have been spent singing carols.

Thirteenth-Century Christmas Plays and Luke in Eight Languages

In Europe, in the thirteenth and fourteenth centuries at Christmas bands of actors went from house to house to give plays telling the story of the birth of Christ. This was how people learned the Bible. The plays were short so that the groups could get to many homes and so that the actors did not have to spend too much time learning lines.

Frederic Karl translated an Austrian play for the freshmen. The Christmas story was different. In

Austria, it was unimaginable an innkeeper would refuse lodging to poor travelers, no matter how full the inn was—hospitality was an unspoken law. In this play, instead of an innkeeper refusing Joseph and Mary lodging, there is a haughty gentleman with a horse and wagon who refuses to pick up travelers. He was played by Laurence with a pillow in his stomach, a turban on his head, shower cloppers on his feet, and a defiant smile on his face. He states in a loud voice that he has no time to stop to pick up travelers and is off on his shower-clog horse. Joseph and Mary—Dick and Helen—continue on their way. The angel Gabriel, Ann, speaks solemnly in explanation. Two angels who follow Joseph and Mary, Jeanie and Elizabeth, speak their parts in unison, blessing the little Christ child and filling in parts of the story here and there. The three shepherds in plain gunny sack clothing were Dick, Charlie, and Gary. Each shepherd brings a gift—milk, a lamb, a woolen coat.

Frederick says the freshmen deserve a lot of credit for preparing the play in two weeks. He just shooed the boys outside into the brush to get shepherds' poles. The white curtains of the Karl's apartment served as clothing for the angels.

During rehearsal, baby Isabel Karl did a fine job as the little Christ child, but before the play, while

Frederick was announcing it, she vocalized her sentiments and had to miss the play.

Following the play, the Christmas story was read from Luke in eight different languages—English by Ralph, French by Ann, Spanish by Judy, Greek by Frederick Karl, Latin by Margaret, German by Miriam, and Japanese by Kenichi. Two guests, a Chinese girl from the Philippines and a Korean girl, students from Iowa City, contributed Chinese and Korean.

We ended with Christmas carols, and our guests, including an Indian student who had been with Gandhi, introduced themselves.

Bah Humbug

For evening Collections, we meet crotchety Ebenezer Scrooge, the tortured and transparent ghost of Jacob Marley, the spirits of Christmas past, present, and future, and Bob Cratchett and his family in *A Christmas Carol* by Dickens.

"Good Morning" in Japanese

At first, Kenichi was slow in English; now he was quicker. We learn "Good morning," "It is a nice day," and to ask "What time is it?" in Japanese. In

Japan, when friends meet, they take off their hats and bow.

Kenichi is fast at ironing because when he was a student, he would iron shirts for friends. Kenichi's father graduated from the University of Michigan and wrote a "First Course in English" for Japanese.

Herberto Sein on Historic 1946 UN Conference

"*Muy buenos tardes*," began Herberto Sein, from Mexico, an Interpreter for the United Nations. Walter McGlenegan of the Des Moines office of the AFSC brought him to us.

Herberto Sein was an interpreter at the historic conference in 1946 when the UN Charter was signed. In spite of some of the trouble behind the charter, because the little nations were willing to trust the big nations, the UN exists today.

The USSR and the US worked together to form the UN. Now they oppose each other in a huge armaments race.

Herberto does not believe war is inevitable as long as people everywhere really want peace. The plans for war are contrary to the Creator's designs. To build a world community, nations must have confidence in each other. One nation must be willing to be the first and trust the other nations.

Seven Ears of Corn

Edgar Anderson talked to us: "Speaking of Corn." He is professor of botany at Washington University in St. Louis and a world authority on corn tassels. Ten years of research on corn has taken him into several Latin American countries. He showed us color slides of village and market scenes and of the plant life observed on his trips.

Each of us eats at least seven ears of corn a day through meat, eggs, and milk. In Mexico, ninety-nine percent of corn is directly consumed. In South America, corn tassels have been regarded as sacred since the Incas. Rarely is there no mention of corn on the newspaper front page.

Our field corn is a mixture of a cream-colored Mexican corn called gourd seed and an Indian corn with long, slender, dark-orange ears called flint. By the middle of the nineteenth century, it was found that this cross was excellent and is the basis of present-day hybrid corn.

Peru has a squatty, fat, conical-shaped ear, which is soaked in water for six months, then hulled, dried, and eaten. It tastes like Roquefort and smells like stale water.

The Iroquois Indians raised sweet corn from Mexico. The Mexicans powdered it and used it as sugar. Since the Incas, it has been used that way on a continent where sugar was scarce. A dark corn, which was not as sweet, was used to eat.

Our golden bantam is a combination of Mexican sweet corn and Indian flint. Five kinds of popcorn were raised in pre-Columbian South America. Western Mexico produced a dark type, while that around Mexico City was white, red, or lavender. Strawberry popcorn, a dark berry-shaped ear, has various uses. Most frequently it is popped but whole ears have been used as hat ornaments.

South American countries, the Balkans, and South East Europe are major popcorn countries. Along the west coast of Chile, it rains only once in seven years, and the people lived only near streams. In a recent excavation near one of these streams, city ruins were found, dating to about 1,200 AD containing many cobs of ancient popcorn. Due to the dry climate the cobs could have been mistaken for popcorn only a year or so old.

Norman Thomas and William McGovern

Fourteen went to Iowa City on November 10, 1952, to hear the Thomas-McGovern debate. "Does the US have a constructive foreign policy?" Norman Thomas, opened the debate, speaking twenty-five minutes; William McGovern, professor of Grand Strategy at Northwestern University, followed, speaking thirty minutes. Thomas gave a five minute rebuttal. The speakers agreed that US foreign policy, although it has good points, needs many changes.

When Walt returned to the dorm, his roommates, Bryan Paul and Danny had rigged up a projector to show slides of Colorado. When Walt opened the door, a string switched on the scenery.

Oyster Supper and Wicked Goldsmith

Supper guests expand our horizons. They tell about the United Nations and international affairs conferences. AFSC workers tell about work camps all over the world. A guest told the life story of Quaker poet, John Greenleaf Whittier, and a historian of science talked about Aristotle, Galileo, and Copernicus. A youth club from an Iowa City church shared ideas from books they were reading.

We had a speaker from the Civil Liberties Union, a speaker about the education of the deaf, and a talk by a reporter on markets on radio and TV from Ames who was a cousin of Leanore.

A professor of education from Iowa State University talked about the US and Communism. A university student told of her experiences during the war in Vienna. A Japanese student answered questions about Japan. Walter Hansen, a West Branch neighbor, showed a shoulder yoke his father had made. He told how his father got the land he now owns and how he built and furnished his home.

Guests bring treats such as ice cream and an oyster supper. Reverend Olson of the Methodist Church in West Branch told of his hobby of making jewelry from sea shells. The Methodist youth group led a discussion of an Indian legend called "The Wicked Goldsmith." Frank Elliot told of his service experiences in Korea. Phillip Hubbard of the Hydraulics Lab at the University of Iowa showed a film describing the laboratory. Reyes Carranza, class of 1951, told of his work camp experience in Jamaica. Myrtle and Wilford Haworth of Cedar Rapids prepared games for Saturday night. Guests from Monrovia, Liberia, and Nigeria talked about culture, religion, politics and education in West Africa. University of Iowa students from Lebanon and the Philippines told about their home countries. A speaker compared Buddhism with Quakerism. John Ofringer, from Holland, was a dinner guest with his wife and daughter.

Alan Balsam, a young Friend from California, visited us for a few days on his way home from two years in Europe working with displaced persons in Germany. In Collection, he told us about the displaced families and their hardship in getting to the United States.

In pre-meeting Collection Rodney Larson spoke about his experiences in Saudi Arabia working with ARAMCO. Alice Barry, Frank Barry's mother, talked about Pine Mountain School in Kentucky where she had been a teacher.

10

Special Events

SCATTERGOOD DAY AND COMMENCEMENT are special times. Students give many demonstrations and presentations. Guest speakers are internationally known Quaker scholars and prominent public figures. "The Building of the Shop" was a presentation that commemorated, in a delightful and highly literate poetry, the marvelous achievement of building the new Shop.

With Pleasing Voices and Great Dignity, "La Cucaracha"

One hundred guests came Saturday, November 29, 1952, for Scattergood Day, in spite of snow and nearly impassible roads. After Meeting, Don Nagler spoke about work camp in El Salvador. Guests watched two soccer games and toured the buildings to see improvements. Isobel Karl demonstrated the potter's wheel.

Students gave a program in the recreation room of the new boys' dorm and rejoiced in plenty of room. The freshmen recited the Psalms 67 and 95 with pleasing voices and great dignity. Lawrence talked about his astronomy project and showed the constellations and planets. Dan talked about bees. The freshmen concluded their part with a lively dramatization of "The Blind Men and the Elephant," the girls soberly chanting the narrative and each boy representing an erring Hindu.

The sophomores sang "La Cucaracha" and homemaking gave a pantomime on table manners, committing various breaches of good manners, and Bryan told them their mistakes through a grate in the wall. English class showed how thirteen Greek roots combine to make twenty English words. Each student held a root and stepped forward to show how that root combined with others to make a complete word. World history did a skit showing how a vassal of feudal Europe paid homage to his lord.

Biology students reported on such projects as Margaret on growing molds, Benetta on identifying insects, Ralph on an indoor garden, Ellis on earthworms, and Betty on her white rats. Betty Jo described the various arts of healing, and Don explained the use of chlorides in preventing tooth decay.

Physics students showed how they calculated where a swinging lead weight would go when cut from its string by Arlene. The weight hit the target and missed the alarm clock suspended right above it. German class recited a poem.

Those who had been at Scattergood twenty-five years ago met in the office to look at pictures, and read messages from those who could not attend.

"The Building of the Shop"

Leanore Goodenow was a director of Scattergood with great vision and ability to inspire. She helped to reestablish the school in 1944. She built the Scattergood, which nurtured so many from the 1940s through the 1960s. An example of her ability to get wonderful products from the faculty and students of Scattergood was "The Building of the Shop" play for a presentation at Commencement on May 31, 1952.

The following are a few lines of the poetry ingeniously composed by faculty members for "The Building of the Shop." This part of commencement met at the incomplete structures of the Shop and Laundry wing. Work such as block laying, nailing sheathing, trench digging, and mortar mixing were demonstrated by students in work clothes, and a chorus and narrators helped the transitions between scenes.

Chorus:
Build me straight, oh worthy students
Staunch and strong, a useful building
That shall laugh at all o'er-crowding
Crafts and laundry both encompass

Narrator:
And the spoken word
With delight the students heard,
And with voices full of glee
They answered "ere long we will build
A structure as goodly and strong and staunch
As ever professional builders launch."
A little blueprint the builders wrought
Which should be to the larger plan
What child is to the man.

Chorus:
Thus they said we shall build this shop,
Lay square the base and plumb the top.

Choose the Durowall with care;
Of all that is unsound beware
For only what is sound and strong
To this building shall belong.

So with the rising of the sun
The excavation was begun.
And soon throughout Scattergood's
bounds
Of shovels and mattocks plied
With vigorous arms on every side;
Plied so deftly and so well
That ere the close of autumn fell
The ditches were dug, the forms
were made.
Then Einor Paulson lent his aid
And Fran began to learn the trade
(block laying)

Day by day the building grew
With timbers fashioned strong and
true
With the plan for the roof that
Douglas drew.
And framed with perfect symmetry
A skeleton roof rose to view

Friends from Ames nailed on the
sheathing
Their unfinished labor leaving
To the work crew
Who amid clamor
Of clattering hammers
Were heard now and then
The song of the work to begin again
Behold at last
The tower rises above the rest.

Special Chorus: Now bring the bell
And lift it high
For placed aloft in the tower
It will please the ear
It will reach the sky
As it peals its greeting far and near
Filling the heart with memories
sweet and endless.
[All the students stand and recite in
unison. While they recite, both bells
ring—the Stavanger bell from the
new bell tower and the old bell from
its stand next to the gym.]
Peal out the bells, those faithful two,
For both are old and both have
served,

And those who heard them have not
swerved
From following the good and true
Let this event our faith renew.

We helped our very talented faculty members to mix concrete and pour footers. We got out of classes to complete the structure before frost. One of the intrepid faculty members did a wonderful balancing act on a narrow plank eventually eighteen feet in the air, each day after classes going higher and higher to complete the bell tower. A drawing in *The Scattergood* showed helpers making mortar according to the formula: "7 of sand, 3½ of cement and water to taste."

A bell from the discontinued Stavanger Quaker School took the place of honor in the new bell tower. When Scattergood's old bell rang from behind the Main Building, a symphony was made with two bells in harmony. A graduate said the crack in the old Scattergood bell ranks it with the Liberty Bell.

The following poems were composed for this occasion. "The Stavanger Bell" was written by a great granddaughter of Nicholas and Lydia Larson.

The Scattergood Bell
The sound of the bell

Is music to my ears.
The sight of the bell
Comforts me within.
The feel of the bell
Makes me feel at peace.
The thought of the bell
Is sweet to my mind
By Caroline Stanley

The Stavanger Bell
Silently it stood
And watched and knew
That sing again it would
On how true
And sweet the tone
That rose and grew
From depths unknown
The peal that broke
The breathless sky
And sent its beauty
Winging by

By Loral Larson

Stavanger teachers and students will be glad
to know contributions to the Bell Tower Fund by
friends of Stavanger total: $182.00. The class of

1896 contributed $60 toward the fund on their fiftieth anniversary, and students and teachers brought the fund to $319.40. Stavanger alumni gathered in the office for a joyous recalling of incidents from school and sharing memories and reading letters from schoolmates. They remembered the sensation of the first pealing of the bell—many had participated in raising funds to eliminate the hand bell.

Faith and Works

Commencement in 1950 was the largest gathering since the re-opening of Scattergood. Anna Brinton talked about Faith and Works. We need to tell others about our ideals, but we must be sure of our beliefs and constantly reexamine them. We need to produce Fruits of the Spirit.

The sophomores presented "The Golden Goose." *Little Red Riding Hood* was given in Spanish by two members of Spanish class with three puppets. The girls' gym class gave a tumbling and rope jumping exhibition, and all joined in folk dancing. Original essays were read by the members of the senior class.

11

The School Farm

THE SCATTERGOOD FARM IS a very important. Every student takes a turn getting up very early to milk the cows and feed the livestock and do it again in the afternoon. When the temperature is ten below zero, we feel very heroic. A new experience for city kids. Besides tending animals, they build hog houses, cut up tree branches, and shovel manure. They see the rhythms of life and help provide food for the school.

Cows Give More When We Sing

Ring! Five o'clock. Time to get up. It's really very hard to get out of a nice warm bed at five in the morning, but chores are calling.

We have to wake the cows up too, and they dislike it as much as we do. Getting up early is such a bother. When they are finally in the barn, they very much enjoy munching their breakfast.

The barn is always humming with sound—pigeons cooing, pigs grunting, a cow mooing, and cat meowing. "Send me a squirt of milk."

They say cows give more milk with music, so I sing. She responds by slapping me in the face with her tail.

A nice thing about Chore Crew—we name the calves. Rough Rocks got her name from the squiggly outline of a white splotches on her back. Never dull, but oh, the sleep we lose!

We Lose Our Beloved Susie, Learn Anatomy, and Gain Block and Tackle

One of the Scattergood family is now a little orphan. She is the daughter of Susie, who we had to butcher after a siege with milk fever and a broken leg. This was a serious loss to the school.

A group went to the farm to help Don Laughlin with the butchering. They spent from 1:30 until 6:00 with skinning while learning about veins and arteries, lymph, and mammary glands, and the digestive system.

A male calf was born to June. Because he was over 100 pounds, a block and tackle were required and was named Block and Tackle. Students were given permission to skip classes observe the operation.

Nine Calves, More Milk, 250 Chicks, and 133 Pullets

Twenty-nine acres of corn yield 2,500 bushels. Three calves were born last week, and we are milking six cows. Livestock on the farm in the fall of 1952 are 59 sheep, 120 pigs, 7 cows and 9 calves. Milk production is way up. New milking machines are faster. Becky preferred the human touch and kicked high and mighty while the milking machine was put on but soon got used to the machine.

We got 250 baby chicks. There were 153 pullets in the newly clean chicken house and show signs of wanting to lay eggs.

Rhode Island Reds and Leghorns Making Babies

In May, we got 250 Rhode Island Red pullets and 20 Leghorn roosters from the Ames In-Cross company. We contract to sell them the eggs from the cross of the pullets and roosters. We get 6 cents a dozen above market price. The chickens from these eggs will be the second cross and will be both good egg producers (a Leghorn quality) and a good meat chicken (Rhode Island Red characteristic).

We made a 50-cent deposit on each bird. Each has a band for which the company will pay 50 cents when turned in. We get $5.00 a month to record egg production.

Hogs, Sows, Piglets, Alfalfa, and Wool

Seventy-five spring hogs are fattening on a home mix APF hog food. Six sows had forty-four piglets, with nine sows yet to farrow. Ten cows give thirty gallons a day. The good summer Alfalfa crop is ample feed and straw for winter.

Fifty western lambs are on pasture and will be sold before winter. We got twenty-five cute lambs from thirty-three ewes, with many twins. Shearing produced 309 pounds of wool, which brought 44 cents a pound.

Two Dead Possums

The farm was in bad shape when purchased. Diligent workers made huge improvements. A new south fence is up after digging out very tough Osage orange trees. Plowing is finished thanks to sunny weather. Harvey Marshall cleaned out the central section of the barn where the haymow goes clear to the floor. He found a cement floor that only lasted a few feet and drug out the old floor boards.

Major renovations include replacing one hundred feet of tile. Two dead possums in the drains were a fun discovery.

Members of Iowa Yearly Meeting tore down fences between calf pens and mangers, dug out the dirt floor, and built a new cement gutter. Don Laughlin built wooden forms for footings. A foundation was poured for an internal wall. New joists and milking stanchions were installed. A cement floor was poured and the room painted white. Several boys enjoy the work and volunteer as often as they can.

12

Quaker Frugality

THE KEY VALUES OF Quakers are simplicity and frugality. Using the earth's resources wisely helps to make nature's bounty available for all of humanity. Frugality at Scattergood keeps education affordable for families of modest means.

Pick Up from Mother Earth—
Wash, Peel, Cook, Can

Gleaning sweet potatoes and corn helps with our food supply. Gleaning capitalizes on the boundless energy and high spirits of teenagers.

After the largest sweet potatoes are harvested, up to six bushels per acre of the small ones remain. Sorting them to pick out the bad ones is important because forty bushels of bruised sweet potatoes would spoil in a week. We stretch out among the piles of potatoes and try to decide whether the lumps are small, large, medium, cut, or rotten, or merely dirty. If engaged in a very interesting conversation and they get into the wrong basket—goodness gracious—they have to be resorted. Eighteen bushels went to attic of the Main Building.

Then washing, peeling, cutting, cooking, and canning. They have appeared as sweet potato pie, sweet potato bread, sweet potatoes mashed, and sweet potatoes baked.

On the last day of corn picking, everyone turned out to glean whatever the picker had left in the field. We divided into teams and worked two afternoons after school.

Five people went to Whittier and picked ten bushels of pears and then went camping. They coated potatoes with mud for cooking in ashes. After dishes, they sang and told stories around the campfire. They got into sleeping bags and attempted to get warm but were cold anyway, so they were up at five to get warm and start breakfast around the campfire.

Nuts, Olives, Smoke-Flavored Cookies

When a grocery store in Whittier had a fire, the damaged stock was purchased by the school. Cream of mushroom and vegetable soup, sardines, Jell-O and a motley items covered the floor of the laboratory. Everything was to be inspected for safety. After the inspectors had pinched, tasted, and smelled the food items, the lab was converted into a can-washing center. Students, loaded with toothpaste, soap, and lemon drops, paid sixty percent off. The only complaint, aside from cookies tasting like smoke, was a toothbrush that fell apart. With so many boxes in the storeroom, you might think we will be eating olives, canned nuts, and tomato soup for a long time. Not a chance with teenage appetites.

Learn Construction, Cut Costs

We economize on costs, and students learn construction, by work on the new Utility Building. It will have a shop, garage, tool room, bell tower, and laundry.

Over the summer, four staff members laid blocks and framed doors and windows. It was amazing to see high walls when we returned. Floors were poured. The school appreciates the help of the West Branch and Whittier communities in lending a tractor and cement mixers. Very, very dedicated Douglas Parker and Kent Erickson spent many hours under an electric light leveling and smoothing the concrete floors before they hardened.

Recycled Elephants

The dining room was a Convention Hall for white elephants. Francis and Barbara Henderson gave each animal an ID, price, and location by desirability. The most popular elephants get table tops; some look down with envy from pipes near the ceiling.

Astounding mix of animals. At 3:30, Monday afternoon tea time, members of the school came. Many got instantly attached to the critters. If the amount in the pocket book was sufficient to cover the fee, what joy. So great was the demand that $20 was collected. The proceeds go to the American Friends Service Committee.

13

Gratitude Attitude

WE NEED TO COUNT our blessings. The generosity of friends of Scattergood is an important way of keeping down costs. Quaker families are especially generous. Businesses contribute with generous discounts. Leanore is a very skilled fundraiser. She inspires with the story of shaping young Quakers in a unique shared-work community. Wonderfully dedicated staff do twenty-four-hour duty. Educational foundations find the unique Quaker story a chance to make an exceptional impact.

Shiny New Green Machines

Nothing could be more thrilling for a teenager than driving shiny new John Deere with manure spreader until . . .

We got a new tractor. It happened after a puncture of one of the big back tires of the Oliver. The tractor was pushing dirt back into a ditch dug for hog watering pipe. The tire hit a lug, causing the fluid to run out.

Replacing or repairing the tire would have been expensive, and the old tractor was undependable—it was better to replace it.

The John Deere Company was approached. A new John Deere for $958.80 in cash. A less expensive 1948 model ruled out. Friends responded, and by week's end, the tractor was endorsed.

John Deere did a twenty-four-hour delivery. The Green Wonder arrived on Saturday November 3. In the haste of delivery, someone left the ignition key on, and a resistor burned out. By noon Monday, the tractor was repaired. It was mandatory to have an extremely rigid inspection by thrilled students.

This new tractor and cultivator have a combined value of $2461.29—an important addition to the farm.

Walt did a test run. He got the Green Marvel and manure spreader stuck in a mudhole. He wrote an English essay about the giant group-hullabaloo to move again.

Gallons of Corn, Sawing Wood

At a school committee meeting, Friends from Paullina brought fifty gallons of corn and a dozen kitchen aprons. The farm committee made plans for a Wood-Sawing Day to supplement fuel at the school.

Light tomato and strawberry crops left the cupboards bare in May. Nearby communities made gave canned food, dried corn, and fresh rhubarb. Friends of Scattergood have given beet pickles, applesauce, potatoes, cabbages, tomatoes, apples, onions, string beans, and much more. Love in action.

Never, Ever, Ever Sweets—Until

We never had sweet snacks on campus, so we were thrilled when we each got a candy bar from Clarence and Eunice Morris. Walter Hansen gave five gallons of honey. Sweet tooth happy.

14

Interest Groups

INTEREST GROUPS PROVIDE A wonderful opportunity for students to explore their talents, develop special skills outside of book learning, and discover new horizons of culture. They strengthen the ties of fellowship and friendship. They also provide the fun needed to contrast with the intensity the classroom.

Drama, Puppets, Farm, Oral Reading, Symbolic Logic, Sewing, Basketry, Music, and More

Interest groups enrich. We meet twice a week. Drama is doing *As You Like It*. Others have done "The Devil and Daniel Webster," a magic act, "Casey at the Bat," and sound effects recalling incidents in the past of the school. A dramatization of "The Monkey's Paw" sent shivers up our backs. A sewing group embroiders pillow cases and makes clothes to send abroad. Oral reading practices to improve expression, enunciation, and volume. Farm science studies agriculture and farm management with Don Laughlin—care and feeding of hogs, sheep and cattle, dairy, and beef. Mutton and wool sheep. We attended a 4-H and Future Farmers of America sheep show in Cedar Rapids. A 4-H Club meets twice a month in the office for business meeting followed by demonstrations of how to prepare nutritious meals. We went to butcher shop in West Branch to study cuts and quality of meat.

A building group works on the new shop. A photography group uses a dark room in the Boys' Dorm. A basketry group makes mats and oblong and round baskets. At Saturday Collection, there were displays by the ceramics and art groups. Symbolic logic group explained their symbols and how they could be used to plan an electric circuit. The singing group sang "Sumer Is a Cumin In" and "English Country Gardens." The model group explained airplanes, gliders, balloons, motors, and locomotives. The Radio group showed what Lowell Thomas's voice must go through before it gets to you. The puppet group did *Rumplestiltskin.* In music appreciation, they learn the difference between "impressionism and expressionism." We listened to Wagner's "The Ring of the Nibelung" and followed the themes for the "Ring," "The Rhine," and "The Rhine Maidens." In "Scheherazade," Sinbad the Sailor, his Ship, the Prince, and the Princess had their own melodies.

A ceramics group meets an hour twice a week. Isobel Karl lets us create whatever we want. She teaches the potter's wheel; a few have made very nice bowls. One of the boys helps Isobel make a kiln. The clay comes from a farm near Earlham, Iowa.

15

Misbehavior

MISBEHAVIOR WAS NEVER SERIOUS—TEENAGE boys and girls, with very active hormones were a volatile mix. No girl ever got pregnant. The staff had a heavy responsibility, however, 24/7. I was very startled, however, at a reunion of four of my classmates of an account of a faculty member catching a freshman girl and senior boy kissing.

At a reunion about forty years after I graduated, I told them that I had had a very, very secret crush on my second cousin, Margaret. Someone said, "Half the guys had a crush on her." I then said, "I wonder what was wrong with the other half." I exchanged annual letter with Margaret for years, and she and her husband got a big charge out of that. She was very vivacious and had been Valentine Queen her freshman year in college in Illinois, remarkable for a modest Quaker lass from Iowa.

With classes, demanding homework, study hall, and everyone having crew responsibilities, there was little chance for serious trouble. We all had a big laugh about a couple who did not hear the "two" (two-minute warning bell) for supper as they were engrossed in ping-pong. They were missed in the dining room and were immediately discovered.

When I was a freshman, it was a lark to sneak out of the Boy's Dorm at night. Freddie Dean and I clambered out of the second floor bathroom window on the fire escape. We just wandered into the corn field. We looked across the campus at the office. Freddie told me that Leanore was always looking out of the office windows at night to detect such antics. We then hurried back up the fire escape so that we would not be detected.

In Closet after Lights Out

A roommate from St. Louis, Tom, would go into the closet at night to read by flashlight after lights out. He stayed at Scattergood only one year, but he visited the school again. He must have had some affection for Scattergood. I found a photo of him leaning on a shovel.

Bryan Paul, Danny, and Walt Camp Out in the Barn

When Bryan Paul and Danny were roommates in the spring of my senior year, and we were on chore crew, we got permission to spend Saturday night over at the barn with our sleeping bags. Bryan Paul and Danny moved the bales about to create tunnels, and I chased them through these tunnels. What fun—we had a great time and slept very well that night, but it was very good to get a hot shower back at school and get the scratchy bits of hay out of our hair.

Picture of Colorado after Lights Out

One evening, the seniors went to Iowa City to attend the Thomas-McGovern debate on American foreign policy. When I walked into our room in the dormitory, I was completely surprised to see appearing on the wall, images of Colorado. Bryan Paul had shown these slides at Collection that night. He rigged our room with a piece of string on the light switch so that when I opened the door, the projector flashed pictures on the wall. I greatly enjoyed the beautiful Kodachrome slides as I loved mountains and photography. We were very quiet so that no one else in the dorm knew. What a blast.

No Beer Bar—Clouds of Dust

When I was a freshman, my second cousin Jim and I decided to bike to forbidden West Liberty. We had no idea what West Liberty was like or how far it was. It was not easy on balloon-tire bicycles with no gears. The gravel roads were very hilly, and cars blew clouds of dust in our faces. It took an hour and a half. When we got there we just rode our bikes around through the downtown without stopping and then returned to campus. If there had seen a beer bar, we would not have gone in. I told no one for *forty* years. My dear wife, Willa, was so intrigued about this that she drove herself over to West Liberty just to see what was there, which was a big *nothing*.

Ich Liebe Dich Means "Pass the Salt"

Miriam and Walt sat at the German table even though we were lowly freshmen and the German speakers were upperclassmen. When Miriam asked how to request the salt from Walt, they told her to say, "Ich liebe dich," whereupon all the German speakers burst out laughing.

16

Nature

We Love Our Bird Friends

WHEN OLD MAN WINTER blows down from the North, bringing the cold, the ice, and snow, we find much of nature is dormant or gone: trees have lost their leaves, plant life has become dormant, and the birds have left for their southern abodes.

At this time of year, from the distant Arctic come birds who find the frosty air and sparkling snow quite suited to their habits and happiness. The plain but handsome juncos, in their stately jackets of gray, come in abundance and fill the air with their happy twitter. Horned larks fly over the snow-bound fields, singing their high tinkling melodies. The red-capped tree sparrows frolic in the barren trees and shrubbery. Occasionally we see a flock of longspurs, with their black crowns, and even snow buntings.

Some birds have been here all summer but endure cold winter. Chickadees, in black cap and bib, merrily frisk from branch to branch, from tree to tree, upside down much of the time, calling to the world in their pleasing *chickadee-dee-dee*. From the top of evergreens, we hear a titmouse, who though dressed in gray, carries a snowy crest on his head and cheers the world with his ringing whistle. On a tree trunk, we find an acrobat, the nuthatch, who walks up and down the trunks of many trees in search of insects emitting his sweet nasal call. The cardinal, in a fine red coat and crest, reminds us that spring is coming in his clear whistle. The noisy blue jays add color and life.

17

Quaker

QUAKER IDEALS SHAPED SCATTERGOOD in ways that were life-changing. Graduates exchange annual letters with schoolmates even after sixty-five years.

Community, Equality, Simplicity, and Pacifism

Leanore articulated Quaker values: community, equality, simplicity, and pacifism.

Community—*everyone* participates in daily work. Although we competed ferociously in sports, there was more emphasis on fellowship than on winning. Every player needs to learn and enjoy. We reveled, however, in beating the alumni on Scattergood Day.

Decisions are made in the Quaker tradition of consensus, not voting. This avoids having an "out group" of members who were outvoted.

Community is strong among Quakers because the denomination is very distinct from mainstream Christianity and small in numbers. Quakers stick together to support each other in a culture that is hostile to their values of non-violence and simplicity. In seventeenth-century England, many died in prison and other Quakers took care of their families. My earliest recorded ancestor, John Blackburn in Armagh, Ireland, was first known from the minutes of the Meeting for Sufferings because the local priest had confiscated a horse in payment of tithes, even though the faraway Parliament in London had banned the practice. He came to Pennsylvania in 1736.

Equality is fundamental. The early Quakers suffered severely for refusing to take off their hats to superiors or swear allegiance to the king. We addressed our teachers by their first names. In the Quaker plain language, the use of *thee* or *thou* instead of *you* indicates equality. In English, technically *you* is plural and an honorific title for superiors. The royal *we* refers to the individual as more than one person. Most students did not use the plain language except with siblings and cousins. In the early years of Scattergood, using *you* instead of *thee* was akin to swearing. Jessie Blackburn Jones, a cousin who ran a dry goods store in West Branch, was widely known for using the plain language with all customers. Quakers were pioneers in the abolition of slavery.

Simplicity was important to the early Quakers to avoid distractions from their attention to God's guidance through the Inner Light. They wore plain dress and avoided demonstrations of material wealth. At Scattergood, girls were encouraged to dress modestly and use makeup sparingly. The boys wore ties, and everyone dressed up for Saturday dinner—a practice for adulthood.

Peace, or harmony and pacifism, is fundamental to Quakers. Since their founding in seventeenth century England, Quakers have stated emphatically that war is against everything that Christ taught.

Children and grandchildren of students and staff from the early days of the school were prominent in the twentieth century Scattergood population and on Scattergood's governing body, the School Committee. Former members of Scattergood were often honored guests. Two of my first cousins attended before I came, and a dozen of my second cousins were students or staff. Uncle Wilmer Young graduated in 1905 and was a guest speaker. I was astonished to get a graduation gift from a great uncle I barely knew. The school had fantastic support from Iowa Quakers who contributed enormous amounts of hard work, skilled labor, equipment, and supplies. They brought extra gifts of food when there were garden crop shortages. Leanore took students to Whittier to pick apples and pears. Newsletters with nationwide distribution enumerated the needs of the school.

Vocation of Friends in the Modern World

For premeeting Collection on First Day, we had three groups. One wrote letters to students in England, Sweden, Switzerland, India, both East and West Germany, Mexico, and Japan.

A group has been reading "Colin Writes to Friends House" by Elfrieda Vipont, and a biography of Elizabeth Fry by Janet Whitney.

A third group discussed "The Vocation of Friends in the Modern World," written in preparation for the Friends World Conference in Oxford in 1952.

Nonviolence Is Active Resistance

Cecil Hinshaw, working for the Fellowship of Reconciliation, said only one percent of the people in India were in complete agreement with Gandhi, but he controlled the nation. Non-violent resistance is not a "do nothing" policy but is warfare by pacifism as active resistance.

He talked about our responsibility to obey laws on March 9, 1953. The juniors and seniors wrote their opinions for English. Emily Post is an authority on etiquette to guide people to live in peace. We must to try to understand laws we do not agree with. If we still cannot agree, we must do something about it. We can refuse to obey the laws and if enough agree, the law may be changed. Government of the people, by the people and for the people.

Traditional Quaker Meeting at Hickory Grove and West Branch

All members of the Scattergood community participate in the traditional Quaker silent worship in the historic Hickory Grove Meetinghouse. It has a divider between the men and women sections, with facing benches for Elders. We all sat on the men's side. In Quaker worship, participants share any message out of the silence they feel will be uplifting.

On Saturday, January 26, 1952, the whole school attended the West Branch Quarterly Meeting (Conservative). The Quarterly Meetings provide inspiration and motivation for all of us and are especially valuable for members of the school not familiar with Friends' manner of conducting meeting for worship and business. The chief business of the meeting was the answers to the queries by the constituent Monthly Meetings. We learn the standards of behavior of upstanding Quakers. "Do we treat all human beings with respect? Do we avoid ostentatious dress and life style? and do we attend worship regularly and punctually?" are a few of the Queries. These teach Quaker values. Friends are to avoid "tale bearing," but gossip (not malicious) seems to an inevitable part of teenage life even at Quaker school. Also was the nomination of Arnold Hoge as Clerk and Eleanor Hampton as Recording Clerk.

We enjoyed a delicious meal with the Friends at the Community House. This was an opportunity for us to acquaint ourselves with members of Iowa Yearly Meeting, many of whom are relatives of Scattergood students.

Wedding in Hickory Grove

The Olive Chamness and Elias Stakland wedding was held in Hickory Grove. The Scattergood community was invited, and most accepted the invitation and a few attended a reception at the home of a local family. Elias is a member of the School Committee.

Quakers from Whittier Saw Timbers

Friends from Whittier spent several days sawing timbers for the roof of the new Shop.

Neighbors Are Regular Guests

Whittier and West Branch Quaker neighbors are regular Tuesday night supper guests.

Friends at Work Today

In Collection, AFSC Work Camps were described by Kent Erickson, who was in work camps in Mexico and North Carolina. Work campers go to work camps for many different reasons but generally find they themselves benefit as much or more than the people they help. Francis Henderson told about foreign service with the AFSC.

Bob Berquist told about the Friends World Committee which helps to reunify the Society of Friends and which planned the Friends World Conference in Oxford, England, in 1952.

The Society of Friends and its organizations are busier than ever in bringing good will and under-standing among different people, as well as within the Society.

Graduates and Harold Attend World Conference

Paul Reece, Virginia Williams, and Harold Burnham attended the Friends World Conference in England in 1952.

Quarterly Meetings

Margaret Boyd, Mary Cope, Rolland Henderson, Eleanor Hinshaw, Ellis Standing, and Harold Burnham slipped off to Bear Creek Quarterly meeting at 5:00 a.m. on March 7, 1953, and then went to Ames where Harold spoke to the Religious Forum at the Friends Meeting.

Four students and two members of Hickory Grove Meeting went to Quarterly Meeting in Stavanger, near La Grande, Iowa. The Stavanger Meeting was formed by a group of Norwegian Friends from Stavanger in the old country in 1864. They withdrew from the progressive yearly meeting in 1885 and joined the conservatives. This community has had a few students at Scattergood.

Universal Military Training Letters

Universal Military Training was the subject of Premeeting Collection. As an English class assignment, the juniors and seniors wrote letters to Congress on the subject.

Whittier Community

Seven students and a faculty member had supper in various Whittier homes before a program in the Community Building. The Scattergood group presented a boys' quintet, two piano numbers, and a puppet show. On May 18, 1953, Harold Burnham and five students visited the Whittier Community Sunday School, attended the Friends Meeting, and joined Friends for lunch and discussion at the home of Dilwin Hampton.

Divide into Group for Premeeting Collection

For premeeting Collection on First Day, we have departed from our regular gathering and divided into three groups.

One of has been writing letters to students of other countries. These include England, Sweden, Switzerland, India, both East and West Germany, Mexico, and Japan.

Another group has been reading stories and selections from "Colin Writes to Friends House" by Elfrieda Vipont and a biography of Elizabeth Fry by Janet Whitney.

A third group discussed "The Vocation of Friends in the Modern World," written in preparation for the Friends World Conference in Oxford in 1952.

18

Recreation

AT A LIVE-IN BOARDING school, there are many choices of recreation in a twenty-four-hour day. Being out in the country provides great opportunities for walking, jogging, hiking, bicycling in the fresh country air, and camping in the woods.

Leanore promoted a snow picnic around a campfire with hot dogs and hot cocoa. The hardy boys who get up before breakfast to jog around the four-mile block receive our admiration. In cold weather the pond is sometimes suitable for ice skating and there are plenty of hills for sledding and skiing. There is no football but plenty of soccer and softball. Basketball in the unheated gym in winter keeps us moving to stay warm. Although there is plenty of competitive spirit, good sportsmanship is emphasized over winning just for the sake of winning.

Folk dancing is a favorite way for shy teenage boys to hold hands with pretty girls.

Red River Valley, Sicilian Circle, Schottish, and the Troika

Folk dancing is eagerly anticipated in warm weather. We learn traditional folk songs and dances of other countries. Many Americans know London Bridge and Farmer in the Dell.

At seven-thirty everyone gathers on the south lawn. Don and Lois Laughlin direct. We begin with the Grand March to warm up. Next is Red River Valley, a simple dance in groups of three. We sing as we do this one. Other favorites are Sicilian Circle, Schottish, and Troika, a very energetic one from Russia in groups of three. Although new students may be clumsy at first, they soon learn and forget themselves.

Folk dancing is great fun and a chance for a teenage boy to hold the hand of a teenage girl without any chance of rejection, and the girls feel the same. We never, ever had couple dancing.

Sign-up sheets are on the bulletin board for deck tennis and badminton.

Good Sportsmanship over Winning

People may wonder why we don't have a larger athletic program at Scattergood nor competitive (intermural) sports. Almost always in competitive sports, ill feelings arise between players as well as between schools. Such an attitude toward other persons and schools is something Scattergood wishes to avoid.

We don't spend a lot of time training to get one good team but spend our time helping everyone learn to play the games. At Scattergood, everyone plays—not just the better players, but everyone. This lets the less experienced get help from the more capable. We play to have fun with a spirit of unity; not thinking, "We have to win."

19

Routine

A ROUTINE EACH DAY helps to get all the chores of daily life done on time. This is important where everyone is dependent on crews to get the food prepared and on the tables for mealtime. Regular crews keep the hot water heaters stoked and the hallways clean.

Every three weeks, students are eager to learn who will be their new table and crew mates. Sometimes we don't know who our classmates will be when different grade levels are mixed to use the skills of our teachers to best advantage, especially for foreign language classes. Special assignments are made, and classes even skipped when labor is needed for work construction projects which depend on good weather. Mid-morning lunch break is a favorite. Breakfast in bed is only a very special irregular event.

Radical Schedule and Seven Student Committees

A new schedule speeds up work on the new shop. The very unusual program will continue until the end of the school year. Some classes meet every other day for ninety minutes. All but three classes meet in the morning.

All regular senior classes except biology have this schedule. A senior taking English, government, Spanish 2, and physics has on one-day Physics for ninety minutes. English for ninety minutes, and class work is done for the day except two days of Bible. The next day is Spanish and Government. Seniors who take biology instead of physics have a study hall during physics and biology in the afternoon.

The juniors have three of four credit courses on this alternating basis and one for forty-five minutes every day, sophomores have two of each kind, and freshmen have all their classes every day.

Afternoons are different. Three classes are biology, geometry, and oriental civilizations. A person divides the time among class, study, work on the shop, in the garden, or on the farm, required organized recreation two days a week, or unorganized recreation. We are very busy. Academic work has priority over volunteer work. Students who do not keep up school work will be in study hall from 1:30 to 4:00.

Seven student committees include Building, Farm, Garden and Grounds, Housekeeping and School Improvements, Dormitory, Music, and Evaluation. A member does not necessarily work on committee projects but helps plan how to get them completed. The Building Committee decides how many can work on the shop at one time and who cleans up. Garden and Grounds chooses plantings and grounds improvements. Farm plans the wood lot preparation for grass. Music plans musical activities. Housekeeping decides when buildings get their grand spring cleaning. Dormitory inspects dorm rooms—untidy students study in the library. ("Walt must improve his housekeeping.") Evaluation Committee examines conflicts and problems and coordinates and makes suggestions. We think all this is a great success.

We Love Midmorning Snacks

Midmorning snacks are ten minutes in the dining room, sometimes with apples or pears, but on a cold, dreary day, hot cocoa warms our toes and refreshes our spirits. A small event, yet very important as a welcome break in a long morning of studies and classes. It brings us closer in a feeling of cooperation and friendship.

Mummies in the Social Room

I get the shock of my life when I see girls wrapped in blankets, lying on the floor like mummies in the Social Room. My first thought, *Scattergood is getting quite a few new things, but I never imagined they would carry it this far and get mummies for our history classes.* I look again and realize it is an afternoon nap. Having discovered something new, I close the door and leave the girls to their peaceful dreams.

Rest Period—Yes or No?

Many boys feel that a rest period is a good thing. We are always very busy, so rest in the afternoon makes us much more effective in our work. We discuss whether or not we want a rest period in boys' house meetings, and we decide that we want one, yet when it comes to carrying out our plan, some of us read and others talk noisily in the bathroom. Frequently, we do not think about what we are doing and come singing or talking up the stairs. Sometimes we crack jokes to each other in the hall.

Do we really want a rest period? Maybe the trouble is that those who don't want one do not speak up enough. But those who want to study could study, and those who wish to rest could rest. But that would prevent the faculty member in charge of study hall from resting. Then, too, those who didn't want to rest would not have a restful atmosphere for the others. Because of this, everyone must take rest period seriously or otherwise no one can. We have decided for everyone to take it, but some of us have trouble in living up to the decision.

No Girls at Breakfast—What on Earth?

A small school allows schedule deviations. One Sunday morning, no girls were in the dining room for breakfast. The two-minute bell rang. Still no clatter or scurrying. Five minutes passed. The girls' dorm was still quiet. Only the seven senior girls were up. Maybe the girls were rebelling against rising the Day of Rest. Maybe they were on strike. Maybe they had sore throats or headaches. Maybe they had stayed up to hear a story or have a pillow fight and had not heard the bell.

Ring! Ring! The "two" rang, calling everyone to breakfast. The boys came obediently trooping in. The girls must have overslept. No. The senior girls

were serving breakfast in bed to all of their com-
rades in the girl's dorm.

When Everything Changes

Mid-January is exciting when everything
changes. Courses change with a new semester. Crew
personnel and table seating assignments change,
and some roommates change. Chore crews change
from girls to boys to deal with colder winds and
deeper snow. A new schedule has an hour period
from 11:25 to 12:25. This last period used to be
forty-five minutes, and this change makes lunch,
and all of the afternoon periods, fifteen minutes
later. This hour period is used for interest groups
two days a week:

Ceramics with Isobel Karl, Art with Frederick
Karl, Symbolic Logic with Kent Erickson, Model
Airplane Building with Don Nagler, Puppet Making
with Joan Erickson and Agard Bailey, and Singing
with Harold Burnham.

New courses are Speech and Latin American
History. The shop class and building crew painted
the dining room. Lunch prep crew has been replaced
by the sophomore class. We hold our collective
breath to see how things turn out when sophomores
fix lunch to apply their knowledge from homemak-

ing. Bryan Michener, Danny Neifert, and Walton Blackburn, the new chore crew, made a good start by neglecting to pull out the lever in their alarm clock the first morning.

20

Staff Members

SCATTERGOOD HAS A VERY exceptional collection of dedicated staff members who strongly believe in the Quaker ideals of Scattergood. They sacrifice their personal time and space to contribute to twenty-four-hour duty. They sometimes take unusual risks to perform work such as building construction. We sometimes need to be more grateful for their commitment to Scattergood.

Narrow Plank Eighteen Feet Up

While it is interesting to watch the progress the construction company makes on the boys' dormitory, we are excited to see the layers of block go higher on the laundry wing and the tower of the utility shop building. Kent Erickson's progress is most noticeable on the tower because it dominates the landscape.

Kent Erickson works on a narrow plank eighteen feet in the air. He faithfully daily goes higher and higher. An errand boy brings him blocks and mortar.

Iris, Wooden Fence, Cement Bench, and Roses

Dedicated faculty improve the campus: Frederick Karl has planted a V-shaped row of iris in the driveway. A heavy wooden fence has gone up between the cottage and the gym. "To keep the snow out," says Kent. Agard built a cement bench in front of the house for a picturesque spot beside the roses crawling over the lattice.

Entirely Too Much Noise, Dictator

The students in ceramics make vases of all shapes and sizes, bowls, cups, casseroles, and plates. Some model human figures or faces. One modeled a life-sized head resembling an unknown animal as a pretense of working the clay together. Mixing the clay is great fun although our teacher, Isobel Karl, says we make entirely too much noise.

The potter's wheel is not as easy as Isobel makes it look. It is really fun, especially when a finger goes through the side of a very special bowl, throwing it around in an interesting shape.

We were sometimes hard on our forgiving faculty. Some of us have guilt for disrespectful class behavior. Leanore later said that she had to be something of a dictator. We were all intimidated by Leanore; we later realize what an enormous challenge she faced with teenagers. We understood how her outstanding leadership made the school a widely appreciated model of Quaker education shared work and community.

In later years, the faculty had more living space, more days off, and more division of labor. When the school was getting reestablished after being a refugee hostel during the Second World War, the endowment was too small to allow specialized staff. The faculty did everything—the farm manager taught science, the dietitian taught homemaking. Faculty members supervised building construction, sometimes spending the wee hours of the morning watching cement harden to be sure it was properly cured. It took a toll on the faculty, but we were extremely fortunate to have such dedicated and understanding teachers. We can hardly overestimate what a contribution they made through their sacrifice of themselves for our sake.

Don and Lois Laughlin Work Hard

Don Laughlin was unstinting in his hard work. He kept old machines in good repair, built seven hog houses, added a new milking parlor, leveled and landscaped the yard around the farm house, built many fences, improved the soil with fertilizer, and taught freshman science including soil conservation practices such as grass waterways, terracing, and crop rotation. Lois directed folk dancing and taught freshman science. The chore crews enjoyed her breakfasts on Monday mornings. She canned fruits and vegetables. We watched David and Janet grow up. When Don left to farm his father's farm near New Providence, we had a farewell looking at slides and reading old logs and paper articles. We wrote mock telegrams to Don and Lois and gave them a waffle iron.

Begonias, Geraniums

The Instruction Building has flower pots with delicate pink tuberous begonias and geraniums. Next to the green leaves are red coleus. In each of the girls' rooms is a cheerful geranium thanks to Bob Berquist, who cares for the garden and flowers during the summer and sees to it that they are indoors in winter.

Bob Berquist a Model of Service, Patience, and Dedication

In the Instruction Building is an array of flower pots, each boasting some flourishing plant, including three delicate pink tuberous begonias, some of the usual variety of begonias, and quite a collection of geraniums. Besides the plentiful green leaves there are red coleus. In each of the girls' rooms is a cheerful geranium plant due to Bob Berquist, who cares for the garden and flowers during the summer and sees to it that they are provided homes indoors during the winter.

Bob Berquist joins in sorting potatoes. All the faculty were very, very committed to everything about community life that they did not hesitate to participate in the most menial work. This is the Quaker value of equality carried to the ultimate.

21

Stories

Quaker Boarding School Out on the Plains of Iowa

WHAT WAS IT LIKE for teenagers at Quaker boarding school in the 1950s? Out in the middle of the Iowa prairie? The average student body was about 40.

My twin sister, Mollie, and I went off to Scattergood School in 1949. Scattergood School is on a windswept hill two miles from West Branch, Iowa. When the temperature is ten below and you get up at five in the morning to go milk the cows, you feel very heroic—especially if you have to milk Buttercup, who tries to put her foot into the bucket. You only get to milk her after you have mastered the art with other cows.

Don Laughlin, the farm manager, has the truck nice and warm for the two-mile drive to the farm, but you race quickly to the milking parlor. The air is warmed by the cows, and you don't even notice the manure smell as you get the warm water to wash the udder. You lean over against the warm side of the cow as she munches her grain and squeeze fast to get done before she finishes her breakfast. You dump the heavy bucket of milk into the separator, which takes the cream off in one stream and the milk in another. You, and your two roommates, get back to school in time for a shower and breakfast with the entire student body—everyone comes to meals unless sick.

At one class reunion, we laughed about the urgent campus search for a couple who thought the two-minute bell was the fifteen-minute bell and continued to play ping-pong.

A devotional passage ends breakfast, and you go back to the dorm to get your books and goof off while the dish and pots crews clean up. Thomas à Kempis, *On the Imitation of Christ*, is heavy stuff for a teenager but is accepted without question as part of life at Quaker school. When I was on pots and pans with Jen, I marveled at how fast she washed and how fast I had to dry. She was the one who had read George Bernard Shaw's *An Intelligent*

Woman's Guide to Socialism and Capitalism to our utter astonishment and admiration.

Knitting Is Contagious

The approach of Christmas may have something to do with all the knitting enthusiasts. Knitting is contagious. It started when Leanore said she hoped we would all find something to content ourselves with during the winter when there is no outside work.

A junior girl appeared in the Social Room one day with a pair of needles and white yarn. She told us she was making a scarf, and other girls soon appeared with needles. Everywhere you now hear click, click, or mumbled talk of directions, "pearl," or "casting off." Scarves, socks, mittens, and sweaters are appearing everywhere. Many fathers will get hand-knit gifts this year. In later years, many of the boys took up the sport.

Too Cold to Milk Cows on a Snowy Morning

A nerve-racking rattling noise shattered the darkness and robbed me of my enchanting dream. I groped around in the darkness for my alarm clock and finally turned the correct knob and ended the racket. Surely we do not have to get up this morning, for how the wind is howling and the bed feels warm. I turned over for a small catnap before getting up. I was on the verge of continuing my dreamland adventures when the light switched on and Don Laughlin gave us a cheery, "Good morning." Don was ready to take us over to the farm to do chores. We shivered as we pulled on our cold chore clothes, but the cold served as a good sleep killer.

Five minutes later, we plowed our way through the snow drifts to where Don had left the pickup. After figuring out which was the front end and which the tail end, we slid the garbage and milk cans in back, and piled into the cab. Since there were three of us, the two underneath usually try to take a nap while the other keeps the windshield clear for Don and dodges the gearshift.

The headlights peer ahead into the flying snow and darkness and make shadows move along the side of the road. We stop at the crossroad to hear ourselves breathe and make sure no other fools are out at this time of the morning.

By the time we reach the farm, we are well awakened by bouncing around the barnyard ruts. Each person trudges off silently in a different direction, stumbling along with an empty milk can or a garbage pail. The barn wakes up suddenly as the beams of light pierce the darkness from the milking parlor windows.

My first job is hashing the pigs. I sneak up to the corncrib with a bucket of kitchen scraps, clamber over the gate, and make an end run for the feed trough. As soon as I bang the bucket against the trough, I hear a dull roar as two hundred hooves scramble across the floor of the hog house, and the pigs burst out of the doors in all directions. Next I slowly fight my way over to the corn crib where I scoop some corn.

The old sows are more polite. Some are waiting for me, but at least one or two are heavy sleepers or do not go to bed at lights out (bedtime in the dormitory), and I must walk out to the hog house, much to the disgust and hunger of the punctual ones, and persuade the sleepers that night is over.

The milking parlor is warmer than the icy air outside. Clarabel, a shorthorn, is dirty as usual. She is the most expensive cow in the barn but seems to love mud better than the others. After a struggle to get the chunky cow to move over I settle down to a steady *swish*, *swish* of milk into the bucket.

After cleaning out the milking parlor, I find Don building a fire under the water fountain to thaw out the pipes.

We arrive back at school just as everyone is sitting down to breakfast, and we must hurry with our deodorization, a good shower.

Help! Help! Help! Quickly Get Buckets of Water to the Woodpile

Loud shouting made me rush to the window to see what the commotion was. Sara Berquist was calling for people to get buckets. Soon to my astonishment, I saw students carrying kitchen pans, waste paper baskets, buckets, and even a garbage can filled with water behind the house.

Then I looked over the fields toward West Branch and saw a cloud of dust. A fire truck was racing toward Scattergood with eight cars following. Up the driveway, the fire truck zoomed and came to an abrupt halt near the woodpile. The men jumped out of the cars and raced for the back of the house.

Betty Hoge popped into the Prophets class to say breathlessly that there was a fire. The class had been discussing the prediction of Israel's destructio, by Amos. Quite appropriate! It was alarming for the arriving members of the School Committee to see a fire truck in the yard and firemen putting out the woodpile fire.

Not Much Fun by Day Two

Lately several people have been sick in bed with colds.

When you are in bed, the first day is fun. In a leisurely way you sleep, rest, and if you feel like it you read a book. You do not usually study.

Between classes, you have visitors from other rooms in the dorm. This is always fun because you can catch up on the news.

The second day comes around and your feelings change slightly. You want to get up. To make this feeling even stronger, you can hear talking downstairs, laughing and singing, plus chairs scraping, and bells ringing, and you get envious of those people.

If you are lucky enough to be sick with someone else, you can sometimes creep down to her room and have a chat with her while everyone else is in class.

Sara comes about three times a day: in the morning, in the afternoon, and at night. When Sara makes a visit it is not always pleasant, even though she has good intentions. You hate cough medicine and hot salt water.

When your temperature is down and you begin to regain your strength you think about getting up.

When Sara says you may get up, everyone soon knows, by gossip. After you have gotten up, you have studies to finish, and crew jobs to pay back. This is the time you wish you had never been sick.

Moral: if you ever want to get sick at Scattergood, I would advise you not be to be sick long.

A Little Talcum Is Always Welcome

Whenever someone has a birthday, we sing to them over supper. Phillip did a major production of making a speech by dashing up to the library, grabbing the portable wooden podium, rushing back down the stairs and setting it up on the table, and then reciting an Ogden Nash poem in full: "A little talcum is always welcome."

Chic Chef's Outfit Helps Pancakes

We observe National Pancake Day. A faculty member appeared in the kitchen loudly demanding pancakes, and soon the rest of us were also. Marjorie and dinner prep crew never worked so hard before, but they stood the strain and kept us supplied with light and crispy pancakes fresh from the griddle. The success of the pancakes was chiefly due to the very chic-looking chef's outfit worn by one of the crew members. Rumor has it that one of the faculty members put away fourteen pancakes.

Out the Window at 4:00 a.m.

We were all sleeping soundly at 4:00 a.m. after an exhausting Halloween party when we awoke to the continuous pealing of the Stavanger bell in the new tower.

"What's up?"

"Fire drill."

"Oh dear, somebody turn the light on."

We put on our shoes and a robe.

"Wonder what time it is?"

"About four I think."

The full moon shone brightly as we clambered out the window and waited our turn to go down the fire escape.

"Last one out, remember to close the window."

We waited at the foot of the fire escape until everyone was safely down. Together we walked over to the office where the girls were to meet us. We were counted. Then we walked back and climbed up the fire escape to our rooms. We were secretly glad it was Sunday, so we had an extra hour of sleep.

A Mouse—Dead or Alive

"What a perfect night for a Halloween party," I said as I looked out my window. The calm October air was unusually warm, and the harvest moon seemed to add spice to the forthcoming fun.

Invitations are found in mailboxes telling students to appear with the Wretched Witches, the Ghastly Ghosts, the Scowling Screech Owls, or the Scraggly Skeletons.

At dinner, we were asked to bring flashlights and time pieces for a scavenger hunt. When the bell rang, people could be seen going to and fro searching for such objects as a black paint can, an armload of hay, a grasshopper, an earth worm, a hardboiled egg, a picture of Truman, a feather, and a mouse, dead or alive. They had an hour and fifteen minutes. One group had everything, including the mouse. One group had caught theirs with a trap, and another other found one under the backstop. Another group had collected everything but the mouse. We were all very ready for hot cocoa and popcorn in the dining room.

Crawl in Silently—Hold Your Breath

I crouched silently in my dark corner and waited. I was seated on one of the dusty two-by-fours in the back of the bike shed. I pulled my knees up to my chin and tried to let my eyes get accustomed to the murky blackness. If I listened carefully, I could hear the stifled breathing of others.

Through the open door, I make out a few stars near the horizon and see gray forms. Suddenly, a black form is outlined in the doorway. It hesitated, then took a cautious step. Then came a loud crash as a stack of hoes and rakes scattered.

I was blinded with a flashlight. Tom had found what he was looking for. He crawled into the corner beside me. There was a whisper from the blackness nearby, asking who had been added.

We were playing Sardines. Four scouts went out to hide, one from each class. After the scouts had gone, each class was to find one. Everyone was to look independently, and no information was to be communicated between hunters. Upon finding a scout, the person would crawl in and wait. This waiting period corresponds to that of sardines waiting to be eaten. The first class to collect all members in a hiding place is the winner.

When the bell rang, the group in the bike shed had all but two members, the group in the root cellar all but three, but neither of the other two scouts had been found. When we counted, we found that one scout had not yet appeared. He was discovered lying on top of a brush pile, not sure whether the game had ended.

Burned to a Crisp

Grinding away is the only way to get done, I tell myself, pausing to rest my aching arm.

"What are we having for lunch?"

I look at my recipe: "F-R-I-C-A-T-T-E-L-L-I."

"Sounds good."

The sophomores take turns being responsible for the kitchen on Mondays. The sophomore in charge makes out the menu and sees that food is prepared on time.

Not so easy.

"Hey, the potatoes are burning dry."

"I don't think the custard will get done in time."

To our relief, we find the potatoes not badly burned and the custard will be done, but will it be just a mite hot to eat?" So much for lunch.

"What shall we have for tea?

"Let's have cookies. I'll mix a batch of peanut butter cookies. You make the ice box kind."

"Sounds okay."

Everything goes along fine until we find we have run out of sugar. "Someone borrow some from Sara."

"Is this all the milk this recipe calls for? It seems a bit floury to me."

"Put more milk in."

"Now it's soggy."

That's all right, put more flour in. Yummy, it sure is good."

"I guess it is ready for the oven. Set it at 300 degrees"

"I'll come back in ten minutes."

(After ten minutes) Sniff. "Oh, terror—they are all burned to a crisp."

It is not always possible to regulate the oven accurately.

"Well, all I've got to say
At the end of the day
I was ready to hit the hay."

Light Makes Smoke, Students Make New Musical Scales

Sit down over here please, where you won't interfere with science but will be able to observe the Scientists. I will interpret the gyrations.

That tall fellow over there, whose hair won't lie down and whose shirt won't stay in, is the director. Those five girls and two boys are the physics class.

Now that you are oriented, I call your attention to what they are doing. I would guess, from the lenses and that big light bulb, they are performing an experiment in light. The bushy-haired fellow is trying to cast an image of the French's bird seed on that piece of paper. The smoke issuing from that table makes me think that heat from the bulb is burning the seed, not casting an image.

The last few days, they have been plucking and banging away, trying to construct a different music scale based on three, four, five ratios, instead of four, five, and six. That probably doesn't make sense to you, but just ask one of them to explain it to you. The other day they measured the distance to the farm by means of a trumpet. They tore all the telephones to pieces, and we couldn't hear anything but physics students and trumpets for two hours.

Rattle-Rattle Goes the Treadle

In the dining room, the whir of the electric sewing machine or the rattle-rattle of the two old treadle sewing machines is sometimes heard when homemaking class is not in session. Once started, a person wants to have a finished product to wear as soon as possible. The sophomore boys are making shirts, bathrobes, or nightclothes. The girls spend their time on blouses or dresses.

As a start, Marjorie, the homemaking teacher, bought the desired colors of shirt material for the boys and blouse materials for the girls. The class discussed the terms used in sewing, and the methods used in straightening and cutting out the pieces of the garment from the material. After we cut out the pieces, Marjorie helped us follow the pattern guides in constructing the garments. Although the girls seem to edge ahead of the boys in their sewing speed, the boys are still just as excited about getting done.

Why Do You Mutter So?

Scene: Scattergood, a room in the dorm. A freshman alone.

Enters a senior, mumbling.

Senior: "Out, out brief candle! Life's but a walking shadow . . ."

Freshman: "Faith, sir! Why do you mutter so?"

Senior: "Marry, I have a piece to learn. Get thee gone and leave me to myself until tomorrow morn . . . a poor player, that struts and frets his hour upon the stage . . ."

Freshman: (aside) "These three nights has he thus muttered. I like not his manner. Mayhap he is mad, but dare not speak." (Exeunt.)

This scene might have occurred when English Literature was learning speeches from Shakespeare's Macbeth. Parts of the play were recorded by professionals. The class compared scenes with our own tape recordings. Some of us promise to be good actors, if encouraged.

22

Weather

THE WEATHER IS IMPORTANT because Scattergood sits atop a windswept hill in the middle of cornfields. We see sky in all directions. The road is gravel and may not be the first to get plowed when heavy snow arrives. The barnyard at the farm gets muddy in wet weather and makes getting around an adventure.

Chicken Tracks

Most agree that spring is here, with warm rain and green grass. Not so with Harold, our science teacher. He says that there are seven more snows to come, and he must know—his system of computation is faultless.

He got this system in Maine. On the day of the first snow, notice the day of the week, the day of the month, and the age of the moon. Add these figures for the number of snowfalls to expect.

No, not all the white substance that falls is snow. A snow is precipitation on which a "chicken track" is visible. Two snow flurries in an hour are not two snows unless it clears up in between.

This sounds fishy, but it works. Listen to the record for three years: Prediction: 33, number: 29. Prediction: 30, number: 31. Prediction: 15, number: 19. In no case has he missed the mark by more than four. This year he predicted 34, and we have had 27. Even allowing for a margin of four, we have tree more snows to expect.

Dust, Dust, Dust—Enough Already

Rain? It has been a long time. In August, we had the last thunderstorm, and now nothing but dust.

If on chore crew, you normally wish for dry. Mud complicates things in the barnyard. By the middle of November, after two and a half months of dry, you are willing to give up comfort and convenience for just a little rain, but preferably a big one.

It came in full force one afternoon when we had almost given up hope. Chore crew cheerfully waded in puddles. There were lakes where all had been bone-dry, drips where drips should not be, and boots where boots had not been before. The Main Building showed its age by leaking in even more spots than last year.

Iowa had been waiting for one good rain. Winter can come in full force as we are ready.

You Never Can Tell

Summer, winter, rain or shine, camping trip, or school day, someone always brings up the weather.

When people come to Iowa, they call Iowa's weather unpredictable. If you want to go camping, you pick a nice dry spell, and sure enough, it rains. You decide to go skiing tomorrow, but in place of snow is bare ground and rain. You decide to paddle a tub on the pond, but by the time you get the tub and paddles, the pond is good for ice skating,

When we feel sorry for ourselves, just think of the poor birds on the first of February when the temperature is almost sixty. Should they start singing or follow tradition and wait until spring? If they are observant, they know it will be ten below zero tomorrow. What a mess this weather, Harold, you can have the job of weather man.

23

Work

WORK IS A KEY element of life at Scattergood. Everyone takes part, even the director. Leanore once went to Whittier to be sure the pear trees had given up all their bounty after students had been over the trees. Everyone works a lot. Leanore teaches religion and the Bible; Don Laughlin, the farm manager, teaches freshman science; and Nurse Sara Berquist manages the crew and table seating assignments.

Two Thousand Quarts of Tomatoes and Forty Old Hens

The sophomore homemaking class and volunteers canned a lot of fruits and vegetables. The spirit of volunteering is so strong that volunteers drop in to work fifteen minutes to three hours.

One year the canned and frozen goods produced at school included the following:

Tomatoes and juice – 2,000 quarts
Green beans – 846 quarts
Corn – 60 gallons frozen
Peaches – 179 quarts frozen and preserved
Cherries – 82 quarts canned
Grape jelly – 15 large jars
Crab apple jelly - 5 large jars

Shelves also include pickles, apple sauce, and plum jelly, which were gifts to the school. Green tomato mincemeat and chili sauce are to come. The sophomores put old hens through a routine for the locker. On three different mornings, they each dressed one hen, making a total of forty.

Blue Jeans Time

Comes May to Scattergood, with its extravaganza of lush green and sprightly party colors, its stir of gentle breezes—and its spring clean-up. No, Scattergood is not exempt from lawn reform.

On May 1, at lunch, Leanore suggested reform. Two new buildings going up on campus and an ambitious winter wind left much picking up, raking, and hauling away to be done. For a job well finished, there would be a picnic in the newly presentable meadow at the farm.

With this lure in mind, we began the cleanup for an hour after afternoon classes. The little heaps of mortar below the walls, left by eager students learning to lay blocks, required energetic pounding, scraping, and raking. The broken pieces of wood from the foundation forms, old lumber from behind the gym, and empty paper cement sacks made a huge pile for a bonfire. The meadow and the grounds were attacked with vigor by capable blue-jeaned folk. The grounds were well groomed by 5:30 so that dinner under the cool maples in the meadow was well deserved.

During spring cleaning, the meal preparation crews cruise the campus to retrieve pots and pans being used for wall scrubbing. Washing third-story windows needs considerable gumption. I lean perilously out the third-story window, my hand clutching a rag and my feet holding tightly to a bed inside the room. The window pane showed one streak where I had managed to wipe off part of the winter's accumulation of dirt, but my ambition left me when I looked at Terra Firma, far below.

At the farm, work is progressing on planting oats, spreading manure, preparing for baby chicks, and building a new stand for the kerosene tank. The largest project was painting the barn. After the cleanup of the wood lot and all the rubbish was removed, grass was planted. Getting the beautiful new John Deere tractor and manure spreader stuck in a mudhole and the project of getting it moving again became an English essay for Walton Blackburn.

Groups biking to Millets Pasture, Todds Park or hiking to East Woods were all home by lunch to continue spring cleaning. The class of 1953 repainted the Hickory Grove Meetinghouse where Graduation is held.

Sheffield Grey for Hickory Grove

On April 27, 1953, the seniors heaved a sigh of relief as they announced that they had finished work on the meetinghouse. Six weeks before, the class looked at the peeling walls and ceiling and decided to take on the project in preparation for commencement and yearly meeting. With the aid of a scaffold, step ladders, ambitious and energetic workers, paint, buckets, rags, scrapers, brushes, and a view of the future appearance of the meetinghouse in mind, we dived into the project. For several weeks the weekly worship was permeated with the smell of paint chips and fresh paint, as the walls, ceiling, and woodwork were scraped and painted.

At first it was exciting to stand on the tall scaffold and wonder about the history of each layer of paint as we scraped away, but soon even the satisfaction of scraping the great flakes off the ceiling became merely a pain in the neck (often literally). Working atop weak-kneed, wiggly step ladders required courage. Classmates steadied the ladders and dodged showers of nasty tasting paint chips. The more vigorous scrapers send showers of paint peelings down on the benches and covers which then have to be swept. But it is fun to chat with fellow workers and imagine how things will look when we are done.

It seemed as if the washing and scraping were endless. Because there was no water at the meetinghouse, the seniors and volunteers carried heavy pails of water down the muddy driveway. After two weeks, the old dirty, peeling paint had disappeared up the chimney in a cloud of dark, strange-smelling smoke, and the white plaster of the walls smiled down in huge, bare patches.

It was a great moment when the first stroke of paint went on the ceiling—Sheffield gray, a light grey that would also cover the woodwork. The walls blossomed in April green, like the trees in the meadow. Once the floor was scrubbed and the scaffold removed, the benches were replaced. Our sigh of relief is quickly followed by a great feeling of admiration.

Rags, Brooms, Scrub Brushes

Before the new wooden bunk beds arrive for the new boys' dormitory, the concrete floors had to be sealed and waxed. A shiny surface makes cleaning easier. The entry way soon was a melting pot of shoes and moccasins of all types as dusty feet were strictly forbidden. A steady stream of persons went to the bathroom to fill mop pails.

Classroom, laboratory, and shop floors receive similar treatment as did the freshly laid oak flooring in the main building lower hall. Waiters traveling between the dining room and kitchen across two planks had to be especially alert lest they meet.

It felt good for nearly half of the school to be helping at once in the utility building preparing for the sealing. Strong backs shift furniture around and vigorous application of detergent to the floors is made with scrubbing and mopping to remove accumulations of grease and grime we had tracked in. I was astonished at the huge number of rags, brooms, scrub brushes, and people in use. These projects can be a time of fun as well as work.

Everyone Pitches In—Pouring Is Fun

Students have a chance to put on work clothes and pitch in on the shop after regular building crews excavated trenches three feet deep and eight inches across for footings. The cement mixing and pouring was done by hand to save the $200 ready-mix charge. In two weeks, the footings were two feet above ground, level with the Instruction Building. Pouring requires patience and exactness, but a lot of fun. Each class spent a whole day to beat cold weather which would crack the cement. Regular crew worked during work periods, with volunteer crews on Monday. Wonderful Quaker neighbors from Whittier and Earlham and elsewhere got the roof on to equip the building for the craft program before winter.

Corners Important

Students and faculty gathered to watch Einer Paulsen lay the cornerstone of our long-awaited shop. He gave advice and started two corners—it's important that corners are well laid. It looked quite simple, but all who have tried their hand understand why a mason is a skilled workman. After the first few days of laying and relaying blocks, we realized we would have to improve rapidly to complete the walls before commencement.

We improve, but the work is slow as we want a well-constructed building. It takes a lot of patience to relay some blocks three and four times, but the result is much more satisfying. A volunteer crew works every school day afternoon and all day Monday. Everyone feels responsible.

Sludge on His Face

On Sunday, November 5, 1950, the septic system on the boys' dorm stopped working. The septic tank was cleaned out and the tiles cleaned and replaced. It turned out to be long and difficult process, but forty members of the community pitched in when it became urgent to get it completed before cold weather. The task of emptying the septic tank was very smelly, but Earl George volunteered to get down into the tank and hand up pails of the smelly sewage. Harold Burnham got a wonderful picture of Earl in the septic tank handing a bucket of sludge up to Tom Blackburn. He smiles up at the camera—gray slime all over his shirt, hat and face

The tiles in the leach field were three feet down. They were dug up, cleaned out and replaced. At one point, wrecking bars and hammers were used to break through the frozen dirt to dig up the tiles as cold nights froze the surface. Each of the exposed laterals had a three-inch layer of fine gravel placed in the bottom of the trench. The clean tiles were then handed down to a worker in the trench and then laid very carefully at exactly the right gradient to carry the flow from the upper part of the tile to the lower part of the leach field. The tiles were then covered with a foot of fine gravel and then re-covered with dirt.

Once the septic system was again ready, the boys were glad they did not have to go to other buildings to use the toilet. The school breathed a sigh of relief that the project was finished just as cold weather was closing in. Everyone is grateful for the wonderful attitude of the community to pitch in with hard work. The fellowship of a common project, and all the silly puns made about sewage waste, made the project memorable. We have vivid memories of a very important project well done without having to hire mechanized equipment or hired labor.

Boom! Crash! I Must Have Fallen, Says Becky

The girls' dorm is quieter while the southeast room is prepared for paint. Instead of dingy brown, we will have acadia green walls and white woodwork. "Timber," says Elizabeth, perched with a bucket of water on a stepladder in front of the door. The door doesn't open any wider, thank goodness, and both bucket and Elizabeth remain on the ladder. An ambitions character makes a sign to "STAY OUT."

We continue sanding, washing walls, and forever scraping until *Boom! Crash!* "Oh dear," says Becky. "I must have fallen." The floor has "met" Becky, who was once above the radiator. After the pieces are picked up, someone calls through a mouthful of peeled paint that it is time to stop.

"Can we move the scaffolding now?"

"No, not yet. I have a little strip left to paint here."

"Hey, I need the thinning spirits over here, my paint is too thick."

"Someone came and took it."

"Go get it, will you?"

"Where is a rag? I got some white paint on the wall."

The junior girls love Acadia green.

Four Cement, Nine Sand, Fourteen Gravel, and Water to Taste

Four shovels of cement, nine shovels of sand, and fourteen shovels of gravel is the formula for cement for the floor of new shop. After putting a bucket of water, the gravel, sand, and cement into the cement mixer, they are transported into the building via wheelbarrow and dumped on the floor. The floor had been leveled and covered with a layer of gravel. After the floor was covered, the tedious task of smoothing a mixture of cement, sand, and water for the final surface begins. This mixture, five shovels of cement, seven of sand, and part of a bucket of water are mixed in a smaller mixer. Then it is smoothed over with great care.

The lintels above the windows are slower and more tiring than the floor. First, a wooden form is built, the cement is then carried in buckets up a shaky ladder to the scaffold, and then poured into the form and smoothed. There is urgency to beat the cold weather.

The materials for the cement come from all over. Sand is from the Cedar River, the gravel from Coralville, and the cement had been stored in Charles Thomas's garage. All fourteen juniors took an afternoon off from classes to pour lintels over the garage entrance and clean and seal the gym floor.

Many Help Prepare for School

Before the beginning of school in 1952, many alumni and students do painting, digging, raking, and washing windows. Faculty, early-arriving students, and even neighbors do gardening, canning and freezing, mattress repair and distribution, laundering, ironing, and floor-sealing. Several people husked corn on the front porch of the old boys' dorm, now called The House while others cut it from the cob in the kitchen.

Section 5

My Personal Faith

My PERSONAL FAITH IS rooted in the teachings of Jesus and my Quaker heritage.

Love Is Central

Love is central to my personal faith and the beliefs of Quakers.

The teachings of Jesus on love are the very foundation of Quaker beliefs. Quakers feel that every thought and act should be in harmony with love:

"But I say to you, Love your enemies and pray for those who persecute you, so that you may be sons of your Father who is in heaven; for he makes his sun rise on the evil and on the good, and sends rain on the just and on the unjust" (Matt. 5:44).

"But I say to you that hear, Love your enemies, do good to those who hate you, pray for those who abuse you" (Luke 6:27–28).

"You shall love your neighbor as yourself. There is no other commandment greater . . ." (Mark 12:31).

A favorite passage of Quakers is 1 Corinthians 13:13: "So faith, hope, and love abide, these three; but the greatest of these is love." The entire chapter 13 is guidance for daily life.

The early Quakers suffered grievously in both England and America for their beliefs. Hundreds died in prison for their refusal to fight for the king nor swear allegiance to the Crown. Whalen reports that "Between 1650 and 1689 more than 450 Quakers died in prison for their religious beliefs, and at least 15,000 spent time in prison" (Whalen, 18).

The New Testament is the basis of the Quaker Peace Testimony: Quakers feel that the way of the Cross of Jesus is entirely inconsistent with war or preparation for war.

We must also *love* (*respect*) ourselves as we "love our neighbor." Just as God loves us without limit, we also must love and respect ourselves.

"There is no fear in love, but perfect love casts out fear" (1 John 4:18).

Be Attuned to the Inner Light

"The Light of Christ Within" or "The Inner Light" is central for Quakers. It is an internal guide. Each member chooses their beliefs. "Quakerism has no theology, no body of religious dogma, no sacred books, no written creed" (Smith 1998).

"Being asked by the Pharisees when the kingdom of God was coming, He answered them, 'The kingdom of God is not coming with signs to be observed; nor will they say 'Lo, here it is!' or 'There!' for behold, the kingdom of God is within you" (Luke 17:20–21). When we pay careful attention, we can call upon Divine Wisdom.

"The Quaker tries to seek direct divine illumination by jettisoning all the Christian sacraments, rituals, hymns, formal prayers, and priesthood. The Quaker tries to live by the Inner Light" (Whalen, 6).

"The Inner Light is not conscience but it is that which enlightens conscience. Quaker theologians usually describe the Inner Light as 'that of God in each man.' People discern the Inner Light when they silently and patiently wait for God to speak to them. Such direct illumination is far superior to the written revelation of the Bible or Tradition of the church, in the Quaker view" (Whalen, 6).

I believe that everyone knows within themselves when they are doing wrong. All the great faith traditions have the Golden Rule. Even secular thought has: "What goes around, comes around." No matter how hard anyone denies it to themselves, they truly do know that harming other people will come back to harm themselves. When we treat others with kindness, forbearance, and forgiveness, they will recognize, whether consciously or unconsciously, that they also can live their lives in a kinder way.

As Dr. Martin Luther King said, "The long arc of the moral universe bends toward justice." Any good deed, no matter how small, makes the world a better place. This is love in action.

Walk by Faith—Just Buckle Right In

"We walk by faith and not by sight" (2 Cor. 5:7).

Sometimes we are unsure of what we ought to be doing to use our gifts in the best way to serve the Lord. Just by getting busy and doing something, we can call on Jesus and our faith to get inspiration.

"When the true intention is to serve God, the path opens."

Once we get busy, further inspiration and inner guidance will come to us.

We can just buckle right in with a trace of a grin.

Obstacles

Sometimes obstacles turn out to be blessings in disguise. Just taking SOME action can open positive opportunities. Just being "good for something" by helping others strengthens us and gives us courage to overcome obstacles. "Just do it." When we get busy, inspiration comes from our Inner Guide. We gain in our spirituality, and in our favor with Jesus, when we act with patience and persistence. Jesus is always ready to help us, but we must ask Him for his help.

Jesus as Close as Our Own Thoughts

Jesus is as close to us as our own thoughts. If we need His help, all we have to do is call on Him with sincerity and belief and He will assist us. In Acts, we read, "In Him we live and move and have our being." (Acts 17:28) Thomas Kelly writes in *A*

Testament of Devotion: "Total preoccupation with the world is sleep but immersion in Him is life." Jesus said, "Lo, I am with you always, to the close of the age" (Matt. 28:20).

"Take time to be holy, Speak Oft with thy Lord, Abide in Him always, and Feed on His word."

Prayer Makes a Difference

Prayer makes a difference. We may enter beautiful houses of worship to pray, but we also make a difference with even the slightest inward prayer for another person. This is uplifting for us and contributes to good health.

We can be in prayer at any time and in any place. We make the world a better place any time we pray for the well-being of anyone. I like to pray: "Lord Jesus Christ, let your healing light and love flow through Willa Marie and keep her comfortable. Lord Jesus Christ, send your guardian angels to comfort, heal, and protect her."

A devotional classic is *The Practice of the Presence of God* by Brother Lawrence. He was as much in prayer while peeling potatoes amid the clatter of the kitchen as when he knelt before the altar.

We should pray for people who annoy us. We should think of their positive qualities as we pray.

I treasure a little book entitled *A Guide to True Peace or the Excellency of Inward and Spiritual Prayer* published by Pendle Hill, the Quaker study center. Howard Brinton, writes, "This little book was written to nourish the spiritual life. Evidently it has succeeded in its purpose, for it passed through at least twelve editions and re-printings from 1813 to 1877. Compiled anonymously by two Quakers, William Backhouse and James Janson, from the writings of three great mystics of a century earlier, Fenelon, Guyon, and Molinos, it was widely used as a devotional book by members of the Society of Friends. Always printed in pocket size, it was constantly ready at hand to plead for 'a species of prayer which may be exercised at all times' (p. 14), 'a lamp continually lighted before the throne of God.' (p. 34) Brinton (the father of a favorite teacher at Scattergood Friends School) writes that when man seems close to success in controlling nature through scientific knowledge, "we stand bewildered in the midst of the ruin we ourselves have created. Many are beginning to doubt whether the meaning and goal of life can be found through power over the world around us, but they know not where else to turn. *A Guide to True Peace* diagnoses our trouble and points out the remedy. It tells us that we are in trouble because, in learning how to control nature, we have neglected to learn how to control ourselves. We must look within, not without, for the meaning and goal of life. In the depths of our being we shall find an inner sanctuary where there is true peace, where all desire for selfish exercise of power is overcome by unselfish love, where the Divine Presence is known by a direct immediate glance of the soul" (Brinton, editor: viii–ix). I carried around in my pocket for years a little cloth-bound copy of this book.

I believe many who search for meaning would treasure *A Guide to True Peace*. When we find peace within, we are more able to create peace around us. When we do good works to help others, we do so with a calm and peaceful spirit.

I love the verse in "This Is My Father's World," which says, "This is my Father's world, oh let me ne'er forget, that though the wrong seems oft so strong, God is the Ruler yet. This is my Father's world, why should my heart be sad, the Lord is King, let the heavens ring, God reigns, let earth be glad."

Let Me Ever Be a Channel of Blessing

A favorite prayer "Lord Jesus Christ, Thy Kingdom come, Thy will be done, on earth as it is in heaven. Lord Jesus, Let me ever be a channel of blessing to all I meet. Let my going out and my coming in be as Thou would have me do."

Go Beyond the Golden Rule

Nothing is more famous than the Golden Rule. "And as you wish men should do to you, do so to them" (Luke 6:31). I believe it is central to all great religious traditions.

Jesus wants us to go beyond the Golden Rule. He taught, "But I say to you, Love your enemies and pray for those who persecute you, so that you may be sons of your Father who is in heaven; for he makes his sun rise on the evil and on the good, and sends rain on the just and on the unjust" (Matt. 5:44) and "But I say to you that hear, Love your enemies, do good to those who hate you, pray for those who abuse you" (Luke 6:27–28).

The Golden Rule leads to peace: "And they shall beat their swords into plowshares, and their spears into pruning hooks; nation shall not lift up sword against nations, neither shall they learn war anymore" (Isa. 2:4).

When we go beyond just treating others as we would want to be treated, we make the world better. The smallest act of love and kindness leads to a chain reaction improving all life on earth.

Law of Karma—What Goes Around

The Golden Rule expresses the law of karma. My concept of karma is that when we do a kind act, we reap a kind act toward us. When we do an unkind act, we reap an unkind act. Paul writes in Galatians 6:7, "Do not be deceived; God is not mocked, for whatever a man sows, that he will also reap."

Jesus states the law of karma: "Judge not, and you will not be judged; condemn not, and you will not be condemned; forgive, and you will be forgiven; give, and it will be given to you; good measure, pressed down, shaken together, running over, will be put onto your lap. For the measure you give will be the measure you get back" (Luke 6:37–38).

As we love our neighbor, our neighbor returns love. In the Lord's Prayer, we pray, "Forgive us our trespasses as we forgive those who trespass against us." We receive forgiveness when we forgive. "What goes around, comes around."

I commend heroic acts—march for civil rights. I believe also that we make the world better with even the smallest act of kindness. A smile, a simple hello can be very uplifting for another.

We never know when even the smallest act can change a life. Here is a familiar story:

"I was walking along and joined a man who seemed very sad. I said, 'Good morning, how are you?' He told me the many troubles he was facing. I listened carefully and then said: 'I hope things get better for you soon.' I learned later that he had been so overwhelmed with his troubles that he had been contemplating killing himself. But my listening to him gave him the courage to face his problems and he decided to continue to live."

Forgiveness—and Ourselves

I believe that forgiveness is central in the great religious traditions: "For if you forgive men their trespasses, your heavenly Father also will forgive you" (Matt. 6:14). In the Lord's Prayer, "And forgive us our debts, as we also have forgiven our debtors" (Matt. 6:12).

Advice counselors tell us that harboring resentment harms our mental health. When we forgive, we are released from a burden.

We must also forgive ourselves. If our heavenly Father can forgive us, we must also forgive ourselves.

Paul wrote, "Beloved, never avenge yourselves, but leave it to the wrath of God; for it is written, 'Vengeance is mine, I will repay, says the Lord'" (Rom. 12:19). Also "See that none of you repays evil with evil, but always seek to do good to one another and to all" (Thess. 5:15).

"Do not return evil for evil or reviling for reviling; but on the contrary bless, for to this you have been called, that you may obtain a blessing" (1 Pet. 3:9).

Judge Not

"Judge not and you will not be judged"—this is a great challenge. We evaluate constantly, but if we look for the good in others and lift them up in prayer, we overcome our tendency to judge. To avoid being judged, we should judge not, as Jesus taught (Luke 6:37). This does not mean, however, that we should not evaluate any situation for danger.

Bear One Another's Burdens

The early Christians had all things in common and helped each other. "Bear one another's burdens, and so fulfill the law of Christ" (Gal. 6:2).

We Each Are Like a Lighthouse

Each of us is like a lighthouse or radio station. Our thoughts radiate throughout the world. When we have positive and kind thoughts, we uplift all humanity. When we have negative thoughts, we are not helpful. I believe that God gave us a mind that we can use to manage our thoughts. When we pray for the well-being of others, we make the world better.

We Are All Connected

I believe that we are all connected with all other people at a deep psychic level. I felt this in a mystical experience when I was seeking an answer to a troubling question. Suddenly, I saw within myself that all life is a beautiful, interconnected whole. Perhaps Jung's "collective unconscious."

When we help another, we feel good about ourselves—positive attitudes foster good health. Even a silent, inward prayer connects us. We are all connected even though we may not be aware.

Meditation

Meditation is a discipline for spiritual guidance and inner peace. It is central to Quaker silent worship. It should be a daily habit. I do find it to be very challenging. Yet it can be extremely rewarding. A widely recommended method is to concentrate on and listen to our own breathing. We should not focus on success in meditation but only to make the effort and let the Spirit guide. A sense of inner peace can be a result, but much patience is required. A national TV Anchor said that even five minutes a day can be extremely helpful.

Mindfulness

Mindfulness is an ancient concept now popular. I am aware, or mindful, of my thoughts and emotions. When I pay careful attention, I ask why something is happening. Once I understand, I am more in control. We can counteract a negative sense with a positive prayer or thought. The power of positive thinking. Positive attitudes benefit everyone.

For Peace, Justice

If you want peace, seek justice.

Gratitude

We need to remember to be grateful for our many, many blessings.

Section 6

Hope for a Better Word-Quakers in the Forefront

THE SOCIETY OF FRIENDS, Quakers, have been in the forefront of social change since their founding in seventeenth- century England. Thousands of them spent time in prison and hundreds died for their faith. My earliest known as Blackburn ancestor, John Blackburn of Armagh, Ireland, was listed in the minutes of the Meeting for Sufferings when a priest illegally confiscated a horse in payment of the tithe to the Catholic Church, contrary to legislation passed by Parliament in London. The husband of Lucretia Mott, renowned American suffragette, is a distant cousin of ours. My grandmother was Mary Mott Young and my brother is Thomas

Mott Blackburn. In 1947 the American Friends Service Committee and the English Friends Service Council, were jointly awarded the Nobel Peace Prize. Smith (1998, xii-xiii) writes that every day brings new public debate over issues Quakers have always addressed: war and peace, social justice, education, health care, poverty, business ethics, public service, the use of world resources. I worked in an American Friends Service Committee work camp in the Mexican village of San Pedro Tlaltenango constructing a school entirely with hand tools. My father, William J. Blackburn, Jr., at age 27, during the flu epidemic of 1918, helped to reorganize the Army hospital at Camp Sherman in Ohio. He would have been promoted from buck private had he not been a non- combatant as a conscientious objector.

Bibliography

Barbour, Hugh and J. William Frost. 1988. *The Quakers*. New York: The Greenwood Press.

Berquist, Robert, David Rhodes, and Carolyn Smith Treadway. 1990. *Scattergood Friends School 1890–1990*. Scattergood Friends School: West Branch, Iowa.

Cooper, Wilmer A.,2000 *Growing Up Plain…New York, Church Publishers, Inc.*

Hamm, Thomas D.,2003 *The Quakers in America, New York, Columbia University Press.*

Hubben, William. *The Christian Denominations.* 1952. Philadelphia, PA: Friends General Conference.

Jones, Rufus M., Isaac Sharpless, Amelia M. Gummere. 2004. *The Quakers in the American Colonies*, University Press of the Pacific: Honolulu, Hawaii.

Lilly, Melinda. *Quakers in Early America.* 2003. Rourke Publishing LLC: Vero Beach, Florida 32963.

Oliver, John W., Jr., Charles L. Cherry, and Caroline L. Cherry. 2007. *Founded by Friends, The Quaker Heritage of Fifteen American Colleges and Universities*. Lanham, Maryland: The Scarecrow Press.

Punshon, John. 1984. *Portrait in Grey: A Short History of the Quakers*, London, Home Service.

Smith, Robert Lawrence. 1998. *A Quaker Book of Wisdom, Life Lessons in Simplicity, Service and Common Sense*. New York: Harper Collins.

Taber, William, Jr. 1976. *Be Gentle, Be Plain: A History of Olney*. Burnsville, North Carolina: Celo Press.

The Holy Bible. 1989. New Revised Standard Version. NY: Oxford University Press.

Whalen, William J. 1991. *The Quakers or Our Neighbors, the Friends*. Philadelphia, PA: Friends General Conference.

Appendix

Shiny New John Deere in Mud

ENGLISH PAPER BY WALTON Blackburn. Junior year, 1952, I was about seventeen years old. My second cousin, Jim Mott, had taught me to drive a tractor one summer when we stayed with his family near Paullina, Iowa, when we attended Iowa Yearly Meeting. I had not yet had any driving lessons on our 1928 Model A Ford in Ohio.

"An Encounter with the Mud, or Extracting Machinery from the Mud"

(Driving the beautiful new green John Deere tractor was a heady experience for a teenager.)

Before taking the load of chicken manure to the cornfield, Harvey Marshall, the farm manager, instructed me to go through the first mudhole on the east side and the second mudhole on the west side. I had to cross the mudhole in order to spread the manure on the corn field, and crossing the mudhole was going to be a problem. Because spring had arrived, the frozen bottom of the mudhole we had been driving the tractor on all winter had thawed. The water from melted snow made the mudhole into a regular creek.

Before taking a load through a mudhole, it is necessary to see where you are going to drive because once you are in the mud going one way, turning the steering wheel does little good. It just slows the tractor.

Somehow, I made the trip through the first mud hold in fifth gear. I turned west between the mudholes, and I almost stopped when I saw the ruts in the second mudhole. The ruts were about half a foot. I kept going, trying to skirt the ruts. A post in the fence on the other side of the deep mud had been removed in order to make more room for getting the tractor and spreader across. I started to cross the ruts cornerwise, and I was going fast enough to make it through when I looked down at my right wheel (the right rear wheel is very large with deep tread—the two large rear wheels are the only ones with power, with two tiny wheels very close together at the front of the engine for steering), and saw that it was going to hit the fence post. I stopped and tried to back up, but the spreader was sitting on the mud instead of its wheels. I was stuck.

The first job is getting the tractor out. It is a good idea to have planks and boards available at your mudhole as aids. We set a plank and a cement block on the mud under the axle of the tractor. We put a jack on the plank and cement block and start jacking up the tractor. The plank sank into the mud because of the suction of the mud on the tire. After we got the wheel a little way out of the mud, we took a plank and tied a rope to one end. We pulled the plank under one tire and repeated the procedure on the other wheel. The tractor's back wheels were now sitting on planks.

Before driving the tractor out of the mud, and before jacking up the wheels, the spreader was unhitched. I gave the tractor enough gas to give it a good start forward and then drove it off the planks. It had a good start and enough momentum and bounced through the mud to dry land.

The next job was getting the loaded spreader out. We made a line from cable, rope, chain, and a wire. On the first try the spreader moved four feet forward in the mud. The wire was the first thing to break. On the second try, the thin rope broke. It was tied together again, and it broke again when the tractor started pulling. Finally, we dared to back the tractor toward the spreader, in hopes that it would pull from that point, without getting stuck.

We were close enough to the manure spreader to connect the cable and the heavy chain. In order to balance the load on the spreader upon the wheels, Earl and Albert got on the back end, almost raising the front end out of the mud.

We learned that once we started with the tractor pulling, we should not throw it out of gear even if it seems like we are going to get stuck because the tractor wheels will eventually reach the bottom of the mud.

The tractor started to skid but slowly it started to move. We waited for the cable to snap, but slowly, little by little, the spreader began to move. As soon as the tractor began moving forward, the spreader started whipping around, almost throwing off the boys on the back end. Now the manure may be spread on the fields.

The next load should be taken to the field by another path.

(1-Book-Grow-Quaker-10-11-16)

About the Author

James Walton (Walt) Blackburn was born in 1935 near Columbus, Ohio, on four acres of land with huge gardens and dairy milk goats. His twin sister, Mollie, is three hours older. Two older brothers are William III and Tom. His father, Dr. William J. Blackburn Jr., taught social work at Ohio State. His PhD dissertation, "The Administration of Criminal Justice in Franklin County Ohio," was published by John Hopkins University. He was raised as a member of the Religious Society of Friends (Quakers), and his parents met at Olney Friends (Quaker Boarding) School in Barnesville, Ohio. His mother, Lorena Young (Blackburn), grew up on a farm near Whittier, Iowa. She attended Westtown Friends School near Philadelphia and Scattergood Friends School near West Branch, Iowa. Her mother, Mary Mott Young, was a relative of the husband of Lucretia Mott, famous suffragist and abolitionist. Grandmother Young started each day with reading Holy Scripture and silent meditation. Her brother,

Wilmer, helped found the American Friends Service Committee, recipient of a Nobel Peace Prize.

Walt and Mollie attended Scattergood Friends School. They went to Quaker Earlham College. Walt dropped out and worked in Mexico building a village school with hand tools. He worked in Paraguay with the Society of Brothers (Bruderhof) and taught high school chemistry and biology in Monteverde Friends Community in Costa Rica. He completed a BA with major in Spanish at Earlham in 1963. He got a master's degree in City Planning at Ohio State and spent two years in the Peace Corps in Iran, conducting a study of the economic demography of the smaller cities of Iran in relation to climatic areas. He completed a master's degree in Professional Studies in International Agriculture at Cornell University and obtained a PhD in Public Administration at Virginia Tech where he married Willa Bruce. They taught public administration at the University of Nebraska at Omaha, and Willa headed a new Department of Public Administration in Springfield, Illinois. Walt worked for the Illinois Department of Human Services. Willa pastored two Methodist churches in Illinois, and they retired in Omaha, Nebraska.

Lightning Source UK Ltd.
Milton Keynes UK
UKHW030827260419
R1880500001B/R18805PG341498UKX9B/1/P